Jonathan Spectrum
The Teleporter

Jonathan Spectrum
The Teleporter

Kenneth Mott

authorHOUSE®

AuthorHouse™ LLC
1663 Liberty Drive
Bloomington, IN 47403
www.authorhouse.com
Phone: 1-800-839-8640

Published by AuthorHouse 09/23/2014

ISBN: 978-1-4969-2601-2 (sc)
ISBN: 978-1-4969-2602-9 (e)

Library of Congress Control Number: 2014916106

Standing in his penthouse apartment; stands the one and only Johnathan Spectrum, the superstar athlete; whom is the world champion in Heavy Weight Boxing, and Professional Football. He is standing there wearing a ten thousand dollar silk lined business suit. He is covered head to toe in expensive designer clothing. He is looking out of the picture pane window on to the snow covered city of Detroit. He is trying to figure out where he is going to go for the winter. He is lamenting his team not going to the championship. "Well there is always next year he thought." He hears the chiming of his cell phone; he looks at it before he walks over to his coffee table and picks it up. He looks down at the caller I.D. display and it is his girlfriend Wanda. He pushes the talk button. "Hello," he said. She said, "Why haven't you called me"? John said, "Well for one, I was thinking and I also just wanted some quiet time." Wanda responded in an aggravated tone but she still kept her composer somewhat, "What do mean quiet time,"? "I am your wife you don't need quiet time from me"! John winced when she made such a strong emphases on 'Me'. John stopped and looked at his phone as if the phone said something to him. "Wanda" he said,

"Baby, you are not my wife, what do you want?" Then it started, this thirty year old woman whom has a master degree in law starting whining like a seven year old child. She said, "I love you, I would do anything for you why do you talk to me like that"? Before John can respond she actually started crying and in her whining voice accused him of cheating on him! Wanda, said, "You got another woman over there don't you". She said "Don't you"! In a hysterical loud voice; sobbing. John stopped talking for a while and walked over to his off white leather couch and sat down and put his head in the palm of his hand as he rested his elbow on his knee. He thought to himself "Why do I put up with this crazy girl. She is such a drama queen"! He actually drowned her out with is thoughts. She screamed over the phone like a child that was being ignored, and in all fairness, he was. He stopped thinking to himself and said; "hey, whoa, whoa, what the hell is wrong with you," "What part of quiet time did you not understand." "I am alone, I am tired of dealing with my fans and my agent's people; do you understand?" Wanda said "Well..." John said in a loud voice; "do you understand?" She 'switched gears'. She went from sobbing to anger in a millisecond. Wanda said; "don't scream at me!" John's brow wrinkled up as he tried to explain and understand Wanda's unusual mood swings. He hung up the phone as Wanda launched into an incoherent babble of rage. Johnathan Spectrum looked at his phone at arm's length and slammed it shut as he could clearly hear "You Black Motherf...".."...! He put the cell phone down on his glass end table and started scratching his head when his cell phone chimed again. It was Wanda of course, and he hit the "ignore call" button. Now back to the question at hand, where do I want to go? John looked around his plush penthouse and walked over to his den and went on line. As he thought "Miami or L.A." his cell phone chimed again. He sighed and it was not Wanda but his agent's number. "I should pick it up," he thought;" my relationship with my agent has not been the same sense we slept together when I had my last fight in Tokyo. John said to himself; "here we go again." Cynthia Porter was my agent and she is a hot one. In more ways than one! She was bi-racial, one of her parents was Latin American and the other was white. John picks up the phone and tried to be as diplomatic as possible. John said "Hi," and it came out all wrong. It sounded like 'Hi, I still want some of that; instead of. "Hi, what's up? Cynthia did not betray any emotions over the phone, if she had any. Maybe she thought us sleeping together was a mistake too. Cynthia said; "Hello John, how have you been we haven't spoken sense we came home"! John said, "Well, I have been okay I was feeling funny about things." Cynthia said "funny, in what way?" Before John could answer there was grunt of someone clearing their throat in the back ground. Cynthia apparently was having some feelings about their sexual encounter, she forgot that they were on speaker phone and there were other people in the room. Cynthia said "Excuse me; John we have Members of the military here who wanted to speak to you." John said "Why?" sitting at his computer in his den/office, trying to figure out why the military would be interested in him? John spoke slowly and deliberately, "O.K. what's up?" Cynthia paused. John he could hear talking in the background and could not make it out. Cynthia said "that he had to come to her office and discuss it, she said; "It was very important we can't talk over the phone." "Wow; John said; "what does the military want with me that they want to talk in private"? John said, "O.K. I'll get down to your office as soon as I can." John said; "give me a couple of hours, O.K." Cynthia said, "O.K. we will see you in a couple of hours"... There was a long pause. She said; "Umm... they want to see you A.S.A.P." John said "O.K. two hours is as soon as possible for me." As if summoned by his voice there was a knock at the door. He got up from his computer desk and walked over to his front door. He looked through the peep hole and saw two men. One white with brown hair tall, over 6 feet and A Latin American man, dark hair, brown eyes, built like a refrigerator. John was standing there looking through the peep hole when another sharp rap of knuckles sounded on the heavy wooden door. John said; "Who is it." He had the cell phone still held to the side of his head when he heard Cynthia say, "That it was men from the government they are there to pick you up." Cynthia said; "John, open the door and let them in". He opened the door and before he could get it all the way open the Latin American agent pushed it open. The Latin American agent said; "I am Agent Rodriguez, sir, you need to come with us." John was looking at them funny and said; "O.K. let me get my coat." Johnathan Spectrum turned around and walked into the bedroom to get his fur coat. John came out of the bedroom after a few seconds, to find much to his chagrin the two agents were walking around this penthouse looking at his expensive furniture and exotic art on his walls. Both of the agents were looking at the one piece of exotic art, it was two women covered head to toe in oil entwined together. It was a very sensual piece of art. Women who have walked into his penthouse would pause and take note of the two women, a black woman and a white woman who were nude and covered head to toe in oil and whose bodies were entwined, and locked into a passionate kiss. John walks up to the agents as they were staring at this one of a kind photo. John said; "hey, fellows, I am ready." The two agents were so engulfed into their own sexual fantasies that they did not hear him as he walked into the room. They both were startled by his abrupt announcement, and looked embarrassed by their lack of poise. Johnathan had a smirk on his face as he looked from both of the agent's faces and saw a combination of shock, and embarrassment. Johnathan Spectrum asked the agents who were they? John said; "Who are you, and who do you represent." The White agent started talking first as they walked toward the door. "My name is Agent Smith"; he said. "We are here to escort you to the General." John looked surprised "What general?" "Hey, what is this about"? "Sir, please relax, everything will be explained to you by the general when we get to the destination." John thought to himself "I don't like the word destination." He kept it to himself; he was the last to leave his penthouse, he closed and locked the door behind him. He heard his cell phone chime, and looked at the caller I.D. display and saw his wanna be wife's phone number; Wanda! John picks up the phone and said; "Yes;" in a neutral tone of voice because he was in the presence of people he did not know. Wanda said; "I am down stairs tell the door man to let me up." John said, "Wanda

I am leaving, I have an appointment, I can't see you now." Wanda said; "I knew it, you up there screwing another woman!" Johnathan walks toward the elevator; Wanda launched into a torrent of insults and threats. She was screaming so loudly that the two agents, Smith and Rodriguez who flanked him looked at each other and kept quiet. Wanda's ranting completely distracted John he did not noticed the helicopter blades as the helicopter flew over the building and landed in the parking lot. Now it was Jonathan's turn to be surprised and embarrassed. Johnathan turned to the agents and said; "hey, man I got a problem." Agent Smith reached into his coat and grabbed something that was hanging underneath his armpit. Agent Smith said; "where's the problem"? John said; "not that type of problem. I got a crazy girl friend." She is down in the lobby and she is going to embarrass me and will try and physically stop me from leaving with you. Agent Rodriguez said; "no problem." They reached the elevator and Smith hit the button for the roof. When Johnathan got on the elevator the cell phone dropped the signal, he sighed and thought to himself "thank God for that". John looked at the two agents and said; "So, where are we going?" Rodriguez said; "the roof, I am going to call the chopper and have it picked us up." John said; "Sweet," as he went up the elevator. He was still thinking about his so called girlfriend." John thought, 'I had sex with her one time." "Why is she so crazy?" John quietly contemplated how he was going to dump her. The elevator made it to the top floor, they walked off the elevator and walked up a flight of stairs to the roof where the helicopter has landed, its blades was chopping the cold winter air. The luxury helicopter that they were going to board was beautiful; it had slick lines and a pointed nose. Johnathan and the two agents approached the helicopter with their heads and backs slightly bent. This helicopter was an executive version and the men could safely walk up to it without bending over. But, Johnathan and the two agents have all been soldiers once, and old habits die hard. Agent Smith opens the door and John got on aboard followed by Agent Rodriguez follow closely by Agent Smith. Agent Smith closed the copters doors the cold air ceased, and the chopping noise was greatly reduced. This model of chopper had tan leather seats and was roomy and quiet. John said; "Do you highly trained and professional men care to enlighten me on where we are going and what we are doing." "We can't tell you because we are not informed nor authorized to speak to you about what going on;" said Agent Smith. John responded with; "spoken like a true company man". Neither agent Smith nor Agent Rodriguez was amused at the last jib. The helicopter disembarked the roof; he wondered what Wanda was doing to the poor doorman. He quickly pushed that memory aside and was having every thought in the world race through his mind, as to why two government agents would pick him up? As John began to think about his unusual dilemma he felt the helicopter touch down and was jolted back into reality. Johns Agent's office was just outside of Detroit, twenty to thirty minutes depending on traffic. John looked at Agent Rodriguez and said; "We here already"? Trying to make small talk; Johnathan began to think why was he as nervous as he thought he was. They touched down; he could see his Agent Cynthia, and a tall white man with a hard looking face. He wore a black beret, a black overcoat; that is commonly worn with class 'A' uniforms. "I am assuming you are the General?" Johnathan Spectrum said, as he walks across the parking lot toward the pair. He said; "I am." He put out his hand; and John took his hand and shook it. The General had a strong grip, brown eyes that looked at him as if he was trying to determine his true value. He looked as if he was in his early sixties, but he was much younger than that, due to stress and actually seeing action. He had a large mustache that was not at army standards, but it was neat all the same. Then Cynthia said; "How was your trip." John looked at her and her facial expressions were unusual, John could not read them. "Probably mixed emotions, because we slept together when we were in Japan," he thought. "Fine," John said. Cynthia and John made brief eye contact and both turned to the General who spoke like he was Zeus, he had such a strong voice it fitted him well; he was a large man who carried a large booming voice. He said; "Lady, Gentleman may we step in out of the cold." The General was constantly looking and watching his surroundings. While Johnathan noticed the General eyes moving back and forth scanning his surroundings; Johnathan felt more nervous. We walked through Cynthia's office building, and Cynthia's fellow agents were staring and pretending not to stare. It felt uncomfortable; "I have been in the public eye now for several years; but this is a different type of something," John thought. John felt like he was being lead to 'gallows' or something! He actually was relieved when he made it to the conference room. The scene was surreal; it was quiet when they walked in. There was his usual team of attorneys that worked for Cynthia, in all past contract negotiations. On the other side of the table, were the general and his team. They were all white males and were all young. There was one Captain and four Lieutenants. Then John noticed an old woman very frail, who had unkempt gray hair, and was wrinkled very badly from old age. She had a cane with a red spot painted on the tip. Even though she had a blind persons cane somehow John felt that she was watching his every movement, and knew when he walk into the room. The oddest thing was the way she dressed. She wore leathers and had tattoos on her neck of a crucifix and a gun scope site. That was unusual to say the least. John said; "How is everybody; he is more talking to his negotiating team than the military personnel. Everybody said; "hi;" of course, but the old lady did not say or do anything. John finally said; "What's up"; "What's with all this 'cloak and dagger' stuff"? The General took his place at the table the military personnel stood at attention when he walked into the room than sat when he sat. The Captain spoke he was a blonde hair blue eyed man he had an athletic physique but did not have that hard edge to his face or swagger that the General had. "Captain James Smith is my name sir"; he said. "We are here to approach you to do some recruitment commercials". Johnathan's smirk was so profound that the General and Captain actually started talking faster and at the same time. The General of course out spoke the Captain with is thunderous voice. The General said; "Hear, us out before you turn us down"! John looked at his Agent Cynthia and Cynthia looked backed at him and hunched her shoulders. The Captain was going on and on about patriotism and loving my country. Then the General said, "You were in the Army before think of all the fun stuff you did." Johnathan faced change from a smirk to a look as if he was constipated. John turns to his agent and said, "Could you take care of this, do I really have to be here"? Just then Johnathan felt a strange feeling like someone was stroking the back of his brain. Johnathan instantly looked at the old lady that everyone else was completely ignoring. Johnathan had a curious feeling; he pushed that unusual feeling he had, out of his mind and kept his concentration on his own thoughts and feelings. He also noticed that the General was studying him a lot more intensely than before. Johnathan actually got up while the Captain was still talking. John said; "please forgive the rudeness, I have a plane to catch and the General stood up and looked from Johnathan Spectrum and back to the old lady who actually starting moving. The old lady had one of her fists balled up and was pounding on her knee in frustration. Johnathan noticed the General's intense scrutiny and the old woman's animation and excused himself and walked out." The Captain was talking as if nothing was happening; he was talking as if he was reading from a script. As Johnathan walked out the General was hot on his coat tails. The General said, "Wait, we had not made an offer yet!" John look at the General and said;" "General, I don't understand, you don't need my presence for a proposal you have my agent who can take care of this for me." Now everyone in the office was looking and listening the other employees had their heads popped up out of their cubicles like prairie dogs pop up out of their holes. John said again in a very low voice; "General you don't need me for this; you and I both know this." There is something going on, I can feel tension, surprise and at the same time, fear and anger." The General facial expressions changed and he regained his composure and military bearing. "O.K., O.K."; John said; "Make your offer leave it with my agent." The General said; "wait, I'll go back with you." John started to wonder what was going on and why is the General acting stupid? Johnathan pulled out his cell phone, as he did so a stretch Limo pulls up. The General opened up the car door, and motioned with his open hand for John to get into the car. John got into the car and General jumped into the car and slammed the door shut. The General was not completely inside in when he said; "drive". The General sat up in the car seat and did not relax. John could not help himself; every alarm in his body was going off! "General, what's going on;" John said? The General was hesitant and started with a sigh. He said; "John you are special". Johnathan Spectrum looked at the General, with a smirk on his face. John said; "I am a super star athlete in professional boxing, and football; of course I am special." Where are you going with this"? The General said; "John, you were under surveillance." Before the General could finish he noticed John's facial expressions. The General said; "Wait a minute, not that type of surveillance"! John said, slightly annoyed; "Well what do you mean"? "That Old Lady," The General said, with up raised hands as to calm John down. That old lady is a psionic or telepath choose whatever title you like." John looked at the General, and his smirk turned into a broad smile. John relaxed a bit, noticeably. John did not say a word to the General. The General starting talking again because he knew skepticism when he saw skepticism; and he read skepticism on John's facial expressions. The General said; "Mr. Spectrum you were invited to a phony contract proposal for a simple telepathic reading"! "What;" John said; "I did not read anything"! "I am not telepathic." "General," John said with a slight chuckle; "What's this really about." The General looked at Johnathan Spectrum slightly annoyed; I said; "We would like to recruit you for a secret government mission. John said sarcastically; "Wow, why didn't you just say that in the first place." "General no thanks," I have too many obligations and commitments." The General said; "John, you are a business man; you have a very unique gift the government will be eager to pay for." John looked at the General and said; "General, I am not telepathic"! The General said; "In a calmer voice trying to defuse the tension that was slowly building. John you are empathic and you have a very rare ability to shut your mind off from psionic intrusion, and suggestion. Johnathan Spectrum looked at the General shocked; "how could you possibly know that"? "That old lady"; as the General started to speak. John finished his sentence, "In the room," John said. "Yeah," the General said slightly embarrassed. John looked at the General and realized he could feel the General's slight embarrassment himself. John did not know he was empathic, he doesn't think he fully knew what that is. Johnathan was sitting there confused and a thousand thoughts rolling through his mind at once. John snapped out of his silent contemplations as he heard the General say; "John your country needs you." John said; "What"? General said; "Your country needs you." John zoned out again.

The General was a low level politician and he was giving his best political speech. John was remotely listening and he heard a voice in his head. (Hi John); John, brush it aside and did not think anything about. The General stop talking and then General heard the voice in his head. John noticed his facial expressions changed and the General was staring at John, he was talking to himself. He was moving his lips slightly and no words were coming out of his mouth. The General blurted out, "Ten million tax free dollars." John was surprised, not at the amount of money but at the tax free part. John was excited and said "OK"! John did not even know what the job was. For all he knew, the General wanted him to go to hell and pimp slap the devil or something. But the General was smiling and was visibly relaxed. Mr. Spectrum we would like to brief you and prep you for the mission at 0800 hours standard time. You will be picked up via limo, not to raise any suspicions and you will be taken to our temporary H.Q. you got it. John said; "O.K."! Tomorrow at 0800 hours." "General please make all my payment arrangements with my agent and all the particulars, like what I like and don't like and what I won't put up with; O.K."? The General said O.K.! The rest of the ride back to Detroit was uneventful and quite relaxing. When John gets back to his building his so-called girlfriend Wanda was still at the security gate whining and throwing an adult temper tantrum. When John got out of the limo, the security guard was relieved and as he looked at John; Wanda turned and looked too. She ran at Johnathan and launch into a torrent of accusations and threats. John turned to Wanda and said; "Why do you come over here every day?" In a meek and calm voice. Wanda said; "What?" in a very quiet and childlike tone. John looked at here again and said it again this time in a clear and commanding voice; "Why do you come over here every day"? Wanda stood there, not looking Johnathan in his eyes. "Wanda"; he snapped! "Why do you come over here every day"? "Jonathan started to walk around her and she said; "I just wanted to see how you are doing". John said; "You saw how I was doing yesterday; what do you want"? Wanda said; well, I am your wife now"... John said; "When did you become my wife"; in a very loud and hostile tone". He said; "You are not going to make me marry you".! "There is no way on 'God's green earth'; I am going to marry a mean, evil, and controlling person like you"! Wanda started to cry and scream; John rolled his eyes and closed them and thought; "<u>Here we go again</u>." She grabbed his arm and John snatched his arm away; as he snatched his arm away she tried to pull his arm close to him and she lost her grip and slipped on the ice and fell into a snow bank, which was piled up two days before, from a snow storm. She lay down in the snow and refused to get up while screaming and yelling that John pushed her. John said; "Jesus, Wanda you're crazy!" John walked away and got into his German Sports car and drove off, the security guard watch him go, he looked back at his crazy girlfriend and then to John and shook his head. While John was waiting at a traffic light he saw an ambulance, and two police cars speed by him with their sirens blaring and lights on. John looked and looked again, and watched as they went into the direction of his penthouse. He said; "I can't believe it, she called to police on me". When the traffic light changed he half wanted to turn around and argue with Wanda, but he ruled against

it and kept driving. He decided that he was going to go to the movies and

kill some time, and thought to himself he picked the wrong day to try and

leave for his off season break.

Chapter 2

As the General rode back to his temporary headquarters, he heard the secure satellite uplink phone ring. The General pulled the phone out of his black over coat. General Clark 'picked up' and said; "General Clark;" As he raised the primary shield. General Clark this is 'controller', General Clark said "Yes, controller." "So what do you think;" controller said. The General said; "He does not suspect he has a rare gift, and he is on board for a large sum of money." The controller said, "How large a sum" The General said; "ten million tax free dollars." The controller paused for a while and then said; "Mr. Spectrum is quite the mercenary." "His payment is larger than what the operation may cost alone." The controller said; "It does not matter, and actually I don't mind a man who has a price." "General," the controller said; "Brief me when you get back to your mobile headquarters." General Clark said; "Will do, Clark out." General Clark called Cynthia, and was slightly relieved but at the same time apprehensive. He was apprehensive about working with a civilian and a man he did not know. While the General thought about what the future may bring. Cynthia; Johnathan Spectrum's agent picked up and she said;

"Cynthia Johnson attorney at law." "Ms. Johnson this is General Clark," the General said. "I would like to inform you Mr. Spectrum and I have made a verbal agreement." Cynthia said; "Oh, he did, well Mr. Clark my client is not going to sign anything without any particulars and until my team and I review any offer that is well suited for my client." "The General was thinking to himself, man, she is a good lawyer." He thought; (she will be the hard one to convince). The General said; "Yes, ma'am, we are well prepared for negotiations, please give Captain Smith all of the particulars of the contract." "Mr. Spectrum and I agree to 10 million tax free dollars". Cynthia paused and said; "Tax free?" Cynthia said; "You really want my client, O.K.". He requires certain things due to his celebrity status, we will not compromise." The General said; "O.K. John and I are meeting 08:00 in the morning; I was going to at least tell him what we wanted for our ten million dollars." Cynthia said; "General, I believe that, that is out of the question." I got a call from the Detroit police they want to question him about an alleged incident outside of his penthouse". The General was surprised and said; "What happened,"? Cynthia fills him in; how John's obsessive girlfriend who is constantly acting likes a child and his trying to get constant attention from him. Cynthia said; "This girl is trying to force John into marriage." "She is trying to make him love her and she is really embarrassing herself." The General said; "Wow, he is a complicated man." Then he said; "don't worry about it, we'll take care of this." Then Cynthia paused over the phone for a while and the General said; "Hello are you still there." Cynthia said; "Yes, I am curious why you would get involve with something I could squash with a few phone calls." The General said; "Mrs. Johnson we need your client's celebrity and reputation intact for this campaign to work." "Please don't take offense but we will take care of this." Cynthia said; "O.K." slowly and said we will meet you at 8:00 am." Ms. Johnson, please let me meet with John alone, trust me it is not business it is strictly informal." Cynthia said; "fine, "I will continue negotiations with your man Smith, good day General." The General hung up his cell phone and was beginning to think. He is going to have a hell of a time with this Wanda, John's so-called girlfriend. He placed a call with the Detroit police and identified himself as Major General Thaddeus Tristan Clark. "To whom am I speaking to?" "This is Sgt. Percy Jones may I help you"? General Clark asks Sgt. Jones the particulars of the given situation. Sgt. Jones told him that Mr. Johnathan Spectrum was involved in a domestic violence complaint by his girlfriend Wanda Jackson. The General said; Sgt. Jones I was with Mr. Spectrum all this morning and I was with him when he alighted my car and got into his. A physical assault did not take place; I was there." Sgt. Jones said; "I see." "We still would like to talk to Mr. Spectrum to verify what actually took place." "Sgt. Jones, there was myself and nine attorneys in the room while Mr. Spectrum was present." Sgt. Jones said; "Well what were you doing"? The General said; "Sir that has nothing to do with you or the Detroit Police." Sgt. Jones became perturbed and said; "I am conducting an investigation." General Clark responded in a calm soothing voice; "investigate what"? "No crime has taken place". Before Sgt. Jones could offered a rebuttal; General Clark said; "You are aware of Mr. Spectrum's celebrity status"? Sgt. Jones said; "I don't care who he is no one is above the law." The General said; "That sir is true." Neither are you; you are required to obey the law like ordinary citizens are." "If you do not you are held civilly and criminally liable for you actions and inactions." There was a pause from Sgt. Jones. The General continued; "Mr. Spectrum is a sports icon and is the pride of your city, which quite frankly cannot afford another scandal." "You Sgt. Jones bring your star athlete up for indictment, when he is clearly innocent." "This would actually end far worse for you and your city than Mister Spectrum". "Do you understand?" Mr. Spectrum was not involved in an alleged incident;" "Do I have to repeat that to you again." "I am calling you to get a handle on this, because the next call I make will be to the Mayor, got it"? Sgt. Jones spoke with a sedated monotone voice and said; "Yes, sir." The General said; "thank you for your cooperation Sgt. Jones you have a nice day."

As the General arrived at his temporary headquarters, which was large customized tour busses. Three to be exact; the outside of the busses looked like regular R.Vs, but on the inside they looked like command control for NORAD. Two of the buses had the General's support staff and the third was his mobile office. When the limo pulled up, the General walked briskly to the side door ran his hand over a security pad and placed his I.D. in the card reader and the door opened. When the General closed the door behind him he noticed the long black SUVs' with security personnel. He wonders how suspicious those black armored plated S.U.V looked. He put it out of his mind when his aide Capt. Morgan approached him for his daily and up to date briefing. Capt. Morgan was a beautiful blonde haired blue eyed woman. Who is the mother of three? One could not tell; she has a body of a very athletic nineteen year old, "General"; Capt. Morgan said. "Yes Captain what it is." Sir, Langley wants an update about Mr. Spectrum. "Oh, tell Langley that Mr. Spectrum is an ally, but an expensive ally." "Captain I have a request that I know they can handle." Mr. Spectrum was accused of assaulting a woman today." Captain Morgan said; "What;" with shock on her face. "Yeah"; the General said; "apparently Mr. Spectrum has a crazy girlfriend." "I am not exaggerating when I say crazy either." "Tell Langley that I have took care of the police but you can never be too sure." "Ask them to do some damage control, the type that will keep our new asset out of jail and off the front pages of every newspaper in the country. "Yes sir," Captain Morgan said; as the General retreated to his secured A.O. He told the captain to give him a secure satellite uplink to Area 51; as the General closed the secure A.O. with and electromagnetic bullet proof door.

The General went straight to his wet bar to load up some Jack and coke: The General took a nice long pull on the drink. He thought to himself, there are a lot of perks with this job. He dropped in a few more ice cubes and poured more Jack in to his cup. His lap top beeped, he looked at the screen; he noticed that it was the satellite uplink that he wanted a minute ago. The General logged on and looked at his lap top screen and noticed that he was in a teleconference with other Generals and the same curiously looking old woman in leathers. "Miss Coleman, I see you have traveled back already," how was your travel." Miss Coleman the old woman

did not sound old at all;" she said; "quick". "The other Generals and a few

suits in the teleconference did note that the general spoke to her first and

did not acknowledge the four star General in the room. The General spoke

first, Major General. The General (General Clark) snapped to attention

in his chair, "Sir." "Tell us about you recruitment of Mr. Spectrum." "Yes

Sir"; General Clark said. "Mr. Spectrum was not as hard as we thought

to come on board." "The General then said; "what is going to cost us."

The hesitation from General Clark was telling. General Clark said; "He

asked for and I agree to" he paused, "ten million tax free dollars," The

General said; "Mr. Spectrum; is a very expensive mercenary". The General

said; "Well, I like a man that can be bought." "That means he is not self-

righteous or too much of a boy scout." Then General Clark spoke again.

"I thought the number was a fair number because Mr. Spectrum makes a

little over $250 million a year due to endorsements and his sports salaries."

The General said; "fair enough, does he know what he is and what we want

from him". This is when the old woman in the leathers, and piercings spoke

up. "Excuse me, gentlemen," she said. Then General McCormick cut her

off and said; "Excuse me, Miss Coleman, I did not mean to cut you off, but

could you identify yourself for the people here that do not know who you

are." She said; "Yes, sir, Gentlemen, I am Beatrice Coleman, I am one of

the very few 'real' telepaths that make up the countries special ops agents."

The few people in the room who did not know who she was had a look of

shock and awe on their faces. The pys ops Agent Beatrice Coleman ignored them and continued. "I was sent with Major General Clark to observe Mr. Johnathan Spectrum whom was born with a strong frontal lobe, and has a natural ability to read people's emotions and to block any type of psychic intrusions. I was regarded as the most powerful known telepath and Mr. Spectrum just simply block my impulsion and he negated my attempt to read his mind; without even trying to." He is truly exceptional, we have psy ops agents who are not as strong as I who was present at Mr. Spectrums title fight and I could not believe how he projected his will on the other fighter in the ring." "We discovered Mr. Spectrum by accident." We should have identified him earlier because it is a rare feat for a man to be a super star athlete in too professional arenas." Mr. Spectrum is a well-rounded person who may suit our interest. He is a running back, and the reigning Heavy Weight Champion of the world." I can fore see him being put in the field and being trained while on the mission." "The mission has a narrow window of an opportunity for success." I think tomorrow when General Clark meets with Mr. Spectrum I strongly recommend that he meets with 'Joe the traveler; that last statement created a stir amongst the suits and high ranting military personnel. One of the suits spoke up. 'Joe the traveler' is an ultra-secret.' I am curious how you know of him and why you think Mr. Spectrum can be trusted with one of our nation's most jealous secret." Beatrice spoke and said; "I know about Joe the traveler like how I know of you." "Mr. Johnson is not your real name. It is the name your Spy master gave you." I am a psy ops agent and I have an ability to see things and hear and sometimes feel things others cannot. This is an ability I was born with, same as Mr. Spectrum, but his God given gifts are different than mine. What makes Mr. Spectrum so important to our little effort? Mr. Johnson said. Miss Beatrice Coleman said; "Well, he has ability to resist psionic control, and his brain is unreadable. Mr. Johnson repeated the last word; "unreadable. Yes, sir. Joe the traveler communicates with telepathy; Mr. Spectrum has a natural ability to communicate using telepathy and has a natural ability to resist any mind attacks or readings. Mr. Spectrum does not have to concentrate his ability it is natural. He, I believe is the only human being besides myself that can have a connection with Joe the traveler without giving away national secrets. Mr. Johnson looked at Miss Beatrice Coleman and said; "could you read my mind"? "Yes," Beatrice said, there was an uneasy commotion the sweep across the room. "Mr. Johnson I can read your mind if I tried to. I have to concentrate and you will undoubtedly feel my intrusions." Now Mr. Spectrum on the other hand cannot read people's minds but he can read emotions he is an empath." "He is an empath and don't know it; well how are you going to brief him and get him up to speed"; said Mr. Johnson. Then General Clark interrupts. Johnathan Spectrum has a strong sense of duty and pride. He is an empathic man who can naturally resist telepathy, but he still is a man." "He has a psychological profile that can be read." He is a very complicated man, which tries to be as uncomplicated as possible." As you well know he is a philanthropist." Mr. Spectrum is building schools in Africa, and donating to many women organizations around the country." "You would admire this guy and think he was a saint; but he is not, he is a womanizer and ruthless business man." "Now here is the complicated part, because he was raised by his Grandparents he is very sensitive of missing, exploited and abused children." He is a millionaire that personally gives nearly 80% of his sport salaries to children's organizations around the world." This guy goes to church but won't hesitate to buy a prostitute." "He is like I said complicated." "O.K."; Mr. Johnson said; "how does this benefit us to know that he is complicated". General Clark said: "with a little deceit and lies here and there, which we are good at we can work the angle with the kids." Mr. Johnson looked at the teleconferencing screen and said; "Just like that, nothing is never that easy." General Clark said; "true, but John is a sucker for kids; trust me we can get him every single time".

****

Jonathan Spectrum just got off the service ramp of the freeway and pulled up into the malls parking lot. He was reflecting on the unusual morning he had. He thought about Wanda but only for a fleeting second. Now General Clark wanted to meet him at 8:00 am because his country needed him. That was a 'crock' he thought he just did not want to be held in low regard, when it came to his reputation. As he thought, he thought about his crazy girlfriend and how is going to spend the 10 million dollars once he got it. "Man, how am I going to get rid of Wanda?" "Man, oh man," he thought about it as he walked through the mall; he stopped to give his fans autographs, and walked to the food court to have a cup of coffee. He was starting to get tired of this celebrity thing. He was constantly smiling and signing autographs since he came to the mall. He thought to his self, I need a vacation; I hope the General picks me a nice hotel and a good place to work out of. He walked through the mall and back to the parking lot, he had a small crowd following him, and he also noticed the two agents who escorted him before in the mall trying to blend in, and doing a very bad job of it. Johnathan Spectrum kept up the facade of smiling and shaking hands and was starting to get annoyed. When he made it to the parking lot he all but ran to his car trying to get away from the crowd of people. When he got to his car there was a business card tucked under one of his wiper blades, he grabbed it and was about to throw it away but he could not miss the strong smell of alluring perfume. He took the card and looked at it; it was just a woman's name and number; he was intrigued so he put the card in his pocket; he waved good bye to his fans that followed him into the parking lot. He got in to his expensive car and drove off. "I got to kill some time," he said out loud. He drove back to Detroit and went in the back way of a topless bar he partly owned. He let himself in the back way and went to his private room that he alone had the key to. He went in to his private suite, and cut on the video audio feed from the rest of the club, and opened up the blinds to a large one-way mirror where he had a very good view of the bar and stage; then he called the bar to send up a girl and some cognac; As he did so, he noticed Smith and Rodriguez walk into the front door: he looked and laughed out loud and said; "enjoy yourselves fellas I am going to be here for a while."

****

At 6:00 am John was awoke by knocking and simultaneous phoning ringing. He looked up and grabbed the phone and looked and the call I.D. display it was listed unavailable he pushed the ignore button and looked over at his Wednesday night girlfriend. She was not awakened by the phone ringing or the knocking at the door. He got up quickly and said; "Who is it in a tired voice;" as he rushed to the door. He looked through the peep hole and saw his favorite two shadows, Smith and Rodriguez. He opened the door Smith and Rodriguez rushed in and there were several other people with them; fifteen to be exact, not including the General and the strange looking old lady in a motorized wheel chair. Before John could say anything General Clark said; "Good morning, we have a high threat priority that requires you expertise." John said; "We agreed to 8:00 am and I don't think that was a good idea also." I should have said 'one-ish' or something." Johnathan snapped out of his half sleep stupor and said; "who are all these people and why are they here?" These people are from Area 51," the General said, as the General spoke John's every Wednesday night girlfriend Julie came to the bed room door. She was wrapped in a bed sheet and was undoubtedly arouse by the talking and the commotion in front room. General Clark look at Julie and said; "Who is that," with one eye brow raised. John looks at him and said "Wednesday"... Uh, I mean Julie. The strange woman in the leather coat said; "She has to get out of here." John said; "Excuse me, this is my house, I am Johnathan Spectrum and who are you." My name is Beatrice Coleman; I am your liaison and your controller." Then Beatrice said more forcefully; "she has to go"! Julie said; "Excuse me I am standing here." General Clark said; "So we noticed." Beatrice turned to Julie and said; "Get dressed and leave." Julie turned like a top and went back to the bed room and closed the door. Beatrice had a strange look on her face. She was already strange but this was a lot different. John could not place it. The technicians were working on an object that looked like a stainless steel trampoline. Five minutes later, Julie walked out of the bedroom; her hair was all over her head like she had a good tumble; and she did get a good one. She looked at John and walked out like she had no control over her legs. Johnathan thought to himself that he never in his life seen Julie get ready so fast, or walk out of the house without doing her hair. John looks a Beatrice and said; "I cannot explain how I know but you did something to her."

Beatrice said; "you are correct." Mr. Spectrum there is a reason why we chose you; we did not pick you by a random lottery." "You have a special God given gift that maybe a handful of people have worldwide." John said; "I am curious, what gift are you referring to and how did you determine I have this so-called gift." "Mr. Spectrum we discovered you had a unique gift of empathy while you were fighting for your title." "That contract negotiation thing was a farce to read you, and to test your abilities." Johnathan was flabbergasted by that omission." John looked back to the General and back to Beatrice and then back again. John said; "so that so called speech about my country needing me was for real." 'Well;' John said; "I don't mean to be a party pooper but, I was not expecting this and seeing how I did not sign anything I am not contractually obligated." The General put both his hands up as in motioning for him to slow down and stop." We have a situation that I think that you could appreciate." "There is a Turk who is selling children on the black market for organ donors." "Johnathan stop talking his jaw was tight. The General continued you are a man who can run a marathon and fight your way out of a of prison riot alone. We need you and your country needs you. John said; "O.K." When do we get started?" One of the nameless techs said; "General the apparatus is ready". Mr. Spectrum just stand on that platform and I will explain everything to you. Johnathan Spectrum hadn't realized that he was still standing in his boxers until now. "Wait a minute; he said." "Let me put something on." "What is this, another test or something."? "The General said; "It would be a lot easier to show you, than to explain it to you." John went into his bedroom and put on some running shoes and a cotton sweat suit. He was looking at his bed with longing eyes. He came out of his bedroom and looked at the unusual thing that was assembled in haste in his front room. John looked a Beatrice and thought "Man she is weird." "O.K. General, I going to do this thing for you; but why do I have to stand on this thing"? The General said; "please John, step up on to the apparatus and stand directly into the middle of it." John said; "O.K. uhh... why General"? The General said; "Mr. Spectrum this is a dry run for a teleporter". John's apprehension left him now, he was skeptical. Johnathan Spectrum stepped up on to the apparatus; and was gone in an instant. Johnathan Spectrum did not feel anything he did not noticed that he was no longer in his penthouse. He was teleported in an instant to a ship in orbit. Johnathan was amazed as he watched the earth slowly spinning in orbit. He simply could not believe what he was seeing. "Yes you are in orbit;" said a voice that sounded like it was computer generated." John felt a very strange mix of emotions fear, excitement, joy, and puzzlement. "Who are you"; John said. The computer generated voice said, "I am Joe". John said; "Joe," the computer generated voice said "Yes, Joe." Joe said; "I am a traveler and I have come from another planet." "Please step down from the apparatus and walk to the middle of the habitat." John hesitated, and said; "habitat", Joe the traveler said; "please forgive me I meant room." As John stepped off of the apparatus, and got good look of the room or habitat it was a dome, just no bigger than a football field. The dome was slightly chilly and when he thought about it, the temperature started to rise. The dome was transparent it was not glass it was of some alien material that can withstand space and extreme temperatures of exiting and reentry of any planet's atmosphere. The floor of the habitat had unusual writing and what looks to be gold and silver filaments inside the floor. There was also a constant back ground noise that sounded like a lion roaring in a distant jungle. After John walked off the apparatus it went flush with the habitat's floor. John looks around as he slowly walked toward the middle of the floor. He kept coming back to the transparent part of the dome that showed him earth spinning on her axis. John walked into the middle of the floor staring and looking around like a lost child. When he walked into the gold and silver filament ring in the middle of the floor; there was an instant flash of light; not so fast that he could not see it; but fast enough to be only a second. As he stood there, an image of what looks to be human to him instantaneously appeared in front of him. It was an obvious replica of what a human being was. The representation was remarkable; but human beings are not blue, and the replica was not breathing, it had no natural movements. John said; "Joe"? Joe said; "yes." You would have thought when a person meets someone from another world that he would have something cleverer to say. "Joe the traveler" started speaking first, John had to step back, and I don't think Joe had any concept of intimate space. Joe spoke without moving his mouth." I am here to ask you for your help. I come from a distant planet, I would not explain where it is or how I came here to your planet because I fear that it will confuse you; but I am here and you are a remarkable creature representing a remarkable species." "I came to your planet, what you call years, many years ago. I have intervened in your existence and in returned I have asked for your help in return. John said;

"intervened in our existence how." Joe had a slight hesitation. Joe said, "I am telling you this because I want you to trust me." John said; "O.K. how did you intervene in our existence. "I helped your people split the atom"; Joe said. "I told Christopher Columbus that your planet was not flat." I have been intervening in your existence for many of your life cycles". You have a word for it, you call it exploiting." John wanted to retort but he could not. He felt a physical presence in his brain. It felt liked someone was actually stroking his brain with calloused hands. Johnathan Spectrum felt it and became angry and the feeling stopped. Joe stopped talking. Joe the traveler stood there as if he was the alien. John said; "Joe how can I help you." John felt a very strong sense of fear and anger. Then he felt unsureness. John said; "Joe, talk to me, what can I do to help you"? There was a long hesitation still as Joe the traveler stood there and did not answer. John said; "I appreciate this experience, this is truly once in a lifetime experience. You don't have to worry about me telling anybody about our meeting I am a very private person. "Joe," John said. "Joe, if you don't mind you can send me back." Joe the traveler, said; "please forgive me; you are the first human beings in your many life cycles that I cannot communicate with telepathically. I am intrigued." "You are truly a remarkable species, it take many species eons to evolve." "Your species are constantly growing and constantly evolving." "I don't think any other sentient species have your rate of development." John raised one eye brow, and said, "Well, uhh can I go or what"? Joe said, "Please don't be so hasty." Stay I have a lot of information to tell you." Joe said; "please," again. As he said please he motioned with his hand and the habitat turned into a rain forest with plush green grass and a small waterfall. It was nice and warm; you can hear the natural sounds of the forest and smell the natural smells. John was amazed again as he looked around the habitat turned into just that and not a room. Joe the traveler began to tell his tale. Obviously he felt differently about his intelligence level and began talking about his home world. He belongs to an extra-terrestrial race that is all but extinct. They are only of few of us left. We are called The Fe-loon; we are a very arrogant and narcissistic race. We live only at the expense of others. Joe the traveler hesitated and said your species were essentially lower than insects to us." John did not say a word he just listened to Joe the traveler as he sat on the cool grass. Joe continued what I am, is a scientist amongst my people, I am not a warrior; I stole our technology and many of our scientific achievements and secrets and hid it from the others of my race." You planet and your people are outside the known universe to my race." I have stolen the Great Universal library and I hid it in your Solar System. Over the years I have fought off psionic invasion and attacks from outside your solar system. I have also directly influenced your history as you know it; much to my distress". Every last one of your incredibly unusual dictators has come from off world. Many of your great wars were fought by higher life forms using your species as combatants." "John was trying to control his breathing but his chest was heaving up and down. John said finally; "I don't believe it." Then Joe said; "It is not hard to believe." "Where did the concept of greed, and slavery come from?" John looked at Joe with an expression of bewilderment and anger." "John"; Joe said; "You got it from us." My race is all but extinct it is no more than thirty of us left. My fellow fe-loons are doing to other planets what we have done to yours." World War II as you knew it was me and my fellow fe-loons fighting over control of your planet using you humans as the fodder." We have used our powers of telepathy to manipulate and exploit your people and world leaders". Johnathan was sweating, and his heart was beating out to chest. He was breathing heavily, as he tried to talk. John finally spoke; "I am out;" you find someone else to use, you are a parasite"! Joe said; "Who?" there is no one else"? Mr. Spectrum you are the most unique human that I have encountered; and I am not just saying that." "You truly are, if you would have been born years early World War II would not have taken place." "I would have used you;" Joe hesitated when he said, used. John did look up at him as he caught the slight inflection in Joe's mechanical voice. "Mr. Johnathan Spectrum"; Joe the traveler said; "you are the only person in the universe that can save your world." "I expect payment!" Johnathan Spectrum said." Joe said; "you are being paid". "I am being paid by my government, and I am working with them. I am not working with you or for you. You are not going to use me either"! I think that we can make an arrangement between you and me and not with that group of N.S.A. people or whoever they are in my penthouse right now. Joe said; "fair enough; what would you want as payment?" John said; "What do you want from me; that will determine the payment; "I want to be well compensated." Joe said; "My concept of wealth is different than yours." all I have is science and, 'technology'"; John finished the sentence for Joe. Then Joe said; "Mr. Spectrum you are truly unique"!

*****

Johnathan sat on the cool green grass as Joe told him about his special request. He wanted Joe to infiltrate a fortress that is being used to as a laboratory to experiment on and splice human and artificial D.N.A. Joe went into vivid detail how this fellow Fe-loon was using humans as cattle. These humans were of all ethnic groups and races but they were from different times during human development before World War II. He said that this Fe-loon fled our solar system with his extra dimensional holding pin. John repeated the words; "extra dimensional holding pin." John had a look of puzzlement on his face. Joe could not read his mind but could read his facial expressions. You know it as an 'ark'. John looked at Joe and said; "You don't mean to tell me that"... before John could finish, Joe said; "yes the very one." Before John could respond, Joe said; "please focus, I will try and explain this to you further; but now is not the time." Joe listens to his briefing of what was expected and how he was supposed to drive off the Fe-loon but not kill it. John said; "I do not understand." The point of this operation is to stop the negative influences and the human experimentation, how am I supposed to stop this "Life-form." He purposely left off the word "higher." Joe said; "that this higher life-form is a Fe-loon like I am and there are not very many of us left. Two of my fellow Fe-loons were killed in Japan by those two crude but effective weapons that I helped create and manufacturer. You help create the two atomic bombs. "Yes," Joe said, there is no day that I do go by that I do not regret how I murdered my fellow Fe-loons. Johnathan noticed no mention of the human toll of the war. John said; "I will drive him off, but if I have to destroy him I would." Joe said; "Is that confidence or arrogance"? John said; "I will not give up my life for an entity that has no regard for me." Joe did not say anything. John said; "I am eager to stop the enslavement and experimentation of my fellow humans tell me what I have to do and when can I get started. Joe did not say anything; he just began to process John facial expressions with the tone of his voice. Joe the traveler had a hard time trying to discern Johnathan Spectrum's demeanor and true intention because he cannot read his mind. Joe was startled at the alarming rate in which humans can evolve. He thought that soon the human race will be the higher life-form. He put that out of his mind for now as he concentrated on the task at hand. Joe told him about a planet in which he referred to as a satellite, in a solar system with no name, and that it is so far from Earth that it cannot be seen by human technology. The planet has no known name, Joe said; but my fellow Fe-loon is there, he is manufacturing weapons and turning that world into his personal laboratory. He has a fortress in the south polar region of the planet and it was chosen because of its remoteness. I have no weapons to give you; you have to take along weapons that your planet has created. John did hear the word weapons, and asked Joe why he needed weapons if he did not want him to kill his fellow Fe-loon. Joe said; the reason why I won the battle between my fellow Fe-loons on this planet is because I used your help, I did not ignore you. Now, my fellow Fe-loon is not going to make that mistake he has manufactured humans with animal

D.N.A. and use these hybrids to control the rest of the population. You will have to use stealth, intrigue, or brute force to fulfill my request. Drive him away do not, kill him. John began to speak again. Joe cut him off and said; "the more we debate the more of your species will be experimented on and exterminated. John said; "O.K. what do you want me to do". Joe said; "we will give you a special suit to wear; so that you can adjust to the different gravity of this particular satellite. John noticed that he said 'We'. Who is 'we'", he said. Joe said 'A^2,' is the artificial intelligence that is a download of your predecessors, Colonel Samuel Sawyer, and Physician Emily Taylor. John look at Joe the traveler and said; "please forgive my ignorance." "What do you mean by downloaded." "Your species have a finite existence I have taken steps to prolong and save many of the most exceptional males and females of your species." "There were others before, but they were lost to the wheels of time." "I have downloaded their likes and dislikes, their wants and needs." "Their feelings and intelligences were recorded and save inside A^2." "A^2 is a living computer and A^2 will be with you as you fulfill my request." "I would like you to transfer to an inter-stellar pod." John said; "inter-stellar pod," more of a question than a statement. "You call them spaceships," Joe said. "This space ship has a natural habitat that will allow you to live in deep space and give you the appearance of your home world." "It has an apparatus for you to teleport back and forth from the pod to the surface." "On the pod you have every manner of weapon created by your kind." "You will need them; the humans on that satellite have been mutated and augmented with animal and alien

D.N.A." "Please, return to the apparatus and you will be teleported to the inter-stellar pod, and your transit will begin." "Johnathan Spectrum was very excited about visiting another world. At the same time he has never been so unsure of himself. He had some military training but he was never black-ops. He was a regular solider though. John walked over to the spot in floor where he first appeared; as he walked toward the apparatus it raised from the floor with no sound. Johnathan look through the Porthole and looked at the Earth with sad longing eyes. He had a bad feeling he was not going to see his home world again. As he contemplated his future as a lower life form he was instantaneously standing on another apparatus. Looking at the earth from another view point; he can see the platform or space station which Joe the traveler spent his life looking down on the earth. The Space station faded away as if it was never there and he heard a man cleared his voice. John turned around and the apparatus room looked like the front room of his penthouse with the exception of a view of downtown Detroit. It was a view of space. He saw standing before him a white man in a confederate uniform, and an Asian woman in a Lab coat and business suit. John look at the two life sized computer generated Icons and said; "A² or Colonel Sawyer and Dr. Emily Taylor." A² said; "yes," the Colonel and the Doctor spoke at the same time. The Colonel said that he was his partner on the ground and said that he was a military man and expected to be obeyed. "I am a southern gentleman, and I don't expect and will not tolerate insubordination from a colored man." A²; said Johnathan, I am a black man from the 21ˢᵗ century I do not take orders from white men. A² said; "You will call me colonel." John said, "I will call you whatever I like". The doctor looked from Colonel Sawyer and Johnathan Spectrum and interjected herself politely and said; "I am here to help you Mr. Spectrum". "Please, welcome aboard the pod, it does not have a name as you can see." We are now moving out of your solar system and we will be teleporting to the satellite that has been chosen for your intervention." John stepped off the apparatus, and did not notice the pod had indeed accelerated and was passing Mars as they spoke. The Colonel said that he was here to help on the ground. "I am here to help you with your strategy and give you practical advice and real time information as it happens. It is imperative that you obey me and listen to everything I tell you." "I know how you blacks are." John said; "excuse me!" Colonel Sawyer said; "you are lazy and ignorant; that was how God made you and I have to work around your obvious handicaps." John look at the Colonel long and hard and said; "Colonel when did you enter the service of our mutual benefactor." "Colonel look at John as if, John spoke to him in a different language. The Colonel did not speak and just looked and John. The trio walked to John's front door and then walked out into a long corridor. Again it looks like his building but the corridor was impossibly long. John turned to Dr. Emily Taylor and said; "I am eager to return to my life, could you tell me how long this may take. The three of them stood in the middle of the corridor; without sound and the feeling of movement the three were moving down the corridor on a conveyor. Dr. Emily Taylor began to explain the physics at work so he can understand them. Emily said, "We are travelling in a pod that ignores space and time as what we as humans know it." Right now we are travelling faster the speed of light, and once we leave your solar system we will teleport via apparatus to the unnamed satellite. It will take a total of 24 hours to travel from your solar system, to the teleport apparatus and the teleport apparatus will teleport this pod to a solar system out of range of the unnamed satellites spy sensors and detectors. We will slowly penetrate the solar system from the moon side of the planet by moving from planet to planet avoiding detection." "Once the pod is in the satellites moon's orbit that is when you will teleport to the surface." Then Colonel Sawyer found his voice and said; "Then I would talk you through your task and give you practical strategies and tactics as you deal with the savages on this unnamed planet." John did not respond to the colonel's remarks; he is a very bigoted man that is a relic from a very dark time of American History. The Colonel is obviously exceptionally brilliant and ignorant at the same time. Mr. Spectrum kept his eyes forward and did not acknowledge the colonel, and kept his questions to a minimum. They finally came to their destination, which looked like a train station. John looks at Dr. Taylor and she saw his expressions of puzzlement and she told him that it was a train waiting at a train station. John was impressed; they were on a walkway conveyor for five minutes at least. Now they come to a train station within the ship. The Colonel said; "What, you act as if you never seen a train." Then he said; "do you require that I explain it to you," in a very sardonic tone and a sarcastic smile. Johnathan stepped on the train and looked for a comfortable place to seat. The train car was truly impressive it had all the creature comforts. The floor was carpeted and had real wooden furniture. The train had a wet bar and nice size refrigerator. As Johnathan sat down the colonel made a point to sit next to him. The colonel said; "I know a lot about Negros and I can control your animal behavior. I own several hundred of you on my plantation. I had a negress as a wet nurse when I was a boy". "Colonel Sawyer", Johnathan said; "I genuinely don't care I am a man who owns not human beings and I am 100 times richer than you. I could say with the utmost confidence that I alone make more money that the entire confederate states combined." The Colonel neck was bulging veins and he was turning red. Johnathan thought that was curious, how this computer program had pride, prejudice and was obvious offended because of his success. Johnathan mused to himself that the colonel was obviously in love with his self and thought that he would be easy to get at. The Colonel recovered from his shock of being put in his place by a black man. John turned to the doctor and said; "Could you please tell me where are we going, and what I will be doing when I got there"? Doctor Taylor said; we are going to the ship's science and medical lab. We are going to download information about the apparatus, the portable apparatus you will be wearing and information about the sentries that will be teleported down to plant surface with." John said; "I did not recall sentries being mentioned and thought I was going in alone." The Colonel could not help not to say anything. The colonel said; "you are not here to practice your limited wit you will be told what you know, and only when you need to know it." John said; "Colonel, I beg your pardon; I understand that you have a superior intellect, but that last question was not for you to answer." "You strike me us being raised in a well-mannered family." The Icon of the colonel was red again and he was staring Johnathan Spectrum in the face as John spoke. John finished his point; "So you know that is inappropriate to interrupt people when they are speaking." The Colonel looked like a lobster where John stopped talking and John turned away from the Colonel and spoke to Doctor Taylor again. "Please, tell me about the sentries, and the downloaded information that I am supposed to receive. The good doctor looked at the colonel who is struggling with being put in his place, and said; "The colonel is more qualified to answer the question about the sentries than I." John said; "O.K., please tell me about the down loads and this portable apparatus colonel". The train was under way and was under way for quite some time. The train was so quiet and smooth that it did not feel like it was moving, but it was. The train closed its doors and started on its destination before the Icons were settled in their seats; it started moving only when John was securely seated. Doctor Taylor began to tell John about his down loads. She said that the down load will consist of the full workings of the portable apparatus. The portable apparatus was a network of millimeter thick and ounce heavy bands that were worn on your ankles, waist, wrist and brow. This apparatus will teleport you from one location to the next; while the ship is in orbit. The portable apparatus would have to teleport you up to the ship first and then back down to the surface. The ship will not rotate in orbit with the planet it will maneuver and stay above your position at all times so you can complete the traveler's request. "Thank, you"; said John; "is there anything else"? Doctor Taylor said; "Yes, you will be down loaded with user knowledge of all your earth's weapons. Now John was surprised his said; "all," incredulously. Doctor Taylor said; "all, we have every manner of weapon from your planet's long history of warfare and violence". "You will be downloaded with an exact inventory of every weapon, its' use and how to maintain that particular weapon". John said; "so I could teleport a fighter jet if I like"? She said; "Yes," "Each weapon would be on the ships inter-demential storage area until you call it down to your hands." John said; "I can just simply say rifle and one would appear". Doctor Taylor said; "it will be teleported to you, it will be teleported directly in front of you and you have to reach out and catch the weapon before it falls to the ground." John said; "I understood." "You will be telepathically linked with us and you think of the weapon that you want, and the weapon via the apparatus, will teleported to you." Vehicle and larger weapons will be teleported to you much of the same way just be mindful of the weight and size of the weapon and the space in which you call it into. John said; "Yes "I understand". Colonel please tell me about the sentries. The Colonel was a very arrogant man, for a computer Icon he was a petty like a child. The Colonel said; "Well, see how you are talking to me now, I will begin and I will talk slowly and use small words so you may understand me." John ignored the colonel's barb. John just thought of his Grandfather Spencer. His Grandfather Spencer told him; "it takes two fools to argue." John just listened intently to what the Confederate Colonel Sawyer had to say."

Colonel Sawyer said; "The sentries are drones, and I control them." John did not miss the strong inflection on the word "I". The colonel continued, "There a 1000 sentry drones that I will send them down as needed. They will be sent down into two places. The drones will be used to back you up and you are vastly outnumbered; but MY superior tactics and combat experience will again prevail." Johnathan could not help but to catch the strong emphasis on the word MY. Johnathan did not respond to the colonels "self-loving" and arrogant demeanor. He wisely let him finish. The Colonel went on for another five minutes or so about the several battles and tight spots he been in militarily. Then the train stopped and they have reached their destination. This ship was truly incredible John thought. When he stepped off of the train he was taken aback by the sunny 80° day that the ship has inside of it. The city in which he saw came straight out of a fairy tale. It was super clean, and despite it being 80° all of the people walked around well dressed in business suits and business attire. The architecture was stunning many of the buildings were glass sky scrapers with different colors of glass. John and the two computer Icons walked to a large building on the pristine street and walked into the lobby. The lobby was plush; the other computer Icons had lab coats on like Doctor Taylor. They were standing in the lobby a mixed array of races and genders. There were a few that were obviously not human and John could not help but to recognize them as so. Johnathan Spectrum never in his life seen an alien before and could not help but to stare at them. Doctor Taylor lead him through the group of scientist; as he walked by them they bowed and gave him there different ethnic greetings that were consistent with their ethnic backgrounds and outer worldly racial groups. John was cordial and had spoken to all the human Icons and nonhuman Icons alike. He walked through the building's lobby that was air conditioned, and took note of the different works of art, stone and other wise. The lobby had leather couches and chairs, species of plants that he could not recognize. John walked across the shiny waxed marble floor, to a large double door. As he walked toward the door and the door opened for him; he entered the room. In the room was a capsule that he knew he was supposed to enter. Doctor Taylor walks with him to the capsule and motioned for Mr. Spectrum to enter as he entered the capsule it sealed around him. As he stood in the capsule the capsule tilted at a forty five degree angle; he felt himself suddenly immobilized as if his body was in stasis but he was awake. Then while lying in the capsule, he started watching the room dissolve and he was standing there alone. He knew that he was not watching a movie but he was directly in the action. John stood in the middle of a bar; a topless bar; at that. When he heard the distinct "zing" of a bullet fly by his ear; He hit the deck without thinking he reacted by reflex alone. Then it occurred to him that he was one of the main characters in this shoot out; and he did not know if he was the villain or hero but he was not going to die. He knew that this was not a simulation but an actual gun fight; the smell of gun powder, and the blood on the walls, from where the bullet missed him and hit one of the unlucky patrons. The piece of trash that took a shot at him was crazy. He was wearing a white silk three piece suit, and white exotic skins shoes. He was walking up right toward were John hit the floor. The whole bar was in an uproar, there were women screaming, cigarette smoke mixing with gun smoke, and people running everywhere. John looked up when he heard three more shots that came from the 9mm pistol that was in the well-dressed gunman's hands. The last shot was the loudest; the bartender pulled out a double barrel shot gun and pointed at the gun man. The bartender lost his life in the effort. The bartender died; while falling forward he pulled the trigger of the shotgun and shot himself with both barrels. The shotgun blast sprayed the wall and ceiling with the bartender's brain and skull fragments. The gunman hesitated not because of the gruesome sight of blood and brains, but because he got his white suit filthy. That's was where John felt he had to act he did not have the opportunity to egress. The gunman was between he and the only door that he can see, and the stage was between he and the bar. John did not see any other option. He thought to himself, either him or me. John looked at the gun man in the strip clubs mirrors and willed a 9mm sub machine gun to his hands. The sub machine gun materialized right at eye level where he is hiding. He had to reach up from the prone position and snag the sub machine gun before it fell to the ground. When John grabbed the sub machine gun, the gunman saw the movement and raised his hand gun and set his body to take his shot. John was already up and had the sub machine gun pointed at him. He thought about it; either it is going to be "him or me". John spoke out loud; "it's going to be him." He went into a low crouching stance when he fired. He fired a small controlled burst. The sub machine gun felt cold in his sweating hands. He pulled the trigger of the sub machine gun it belched out a foot of fire from the muzzle. John looked at the gunman and watched him as he died where he stood. It all unfolded in slow motion right before his eyes. He looked at every hole as it exploded in the gun man's body. How his eyes were full of shock and awe and faded into lifelessness. The gunman's white suit was soaked in his blood; as the recoil from the sub machine gun raised the muzzle with every shot. That's how the bullet holes in his gun man's chest were; John's burst was short and a total of five bullets left the gun, but all the bullets struck home. The first three were in the middle of his chest and the last two went up, one in the throat and the last on in the chin. He was lifeless and his body fell straight down to the ground like a boneless fish. John looked around the strip club where there were people hiding under tables and peeking around corners, at him. The atmosphere was unreal, the strobe lights were pulsating and the crappy music was still playing. John was suddenly brought back into reality by the faint but distinct sounds of police sirens. He wills his hands empty, and the sub machine gun teleported away. As he made his way to the door, two of the bars employees, possibly two more bouncers moved to try and intercept him as he retreated from the crime scene. One of the guys was huge, he was a big black bald guy with slacks, nice leather shoes, and his belt was holding on for dear life, this guy had to be the better part of 400 pounds. He had on a black T-shirt that showed his stocky shoulders and arms as well as his quadruple-x belly. The other guy was a small framed wiry looking guy. He had on tight blue jeans that showed off his moose knuckle. He was wearing a T-shirt with no logo or design. He had an old cowboy hat that hid his uncut long hair. John looked at the two of them and looked at the cowboy. He knew that he was going to have more trouble from him than from Mr. 400 pounds. Sure enough the cowboy was quick on the draw. He launched into a one-two combination than surprised John and stunned him when he was hit in the head by the cowboy's quick hands. John stumbled back, as he tasted the salty blood from his nose. The two of them looked a John and showed their teeth the 400 pound bouncer had a gold grill in his mouth. He looked rather ridiculous he was a dark skinned black man and he had a gold grill that when he smiled he looked like a freight train coming down a tunnel. The cowboy had chaw in his mouth, and smiles at John just the same but kept his mouth closed. Then it was Johns turn to smile back. John thought to his self 'I am a professional and he is an amateur'. The two bouncers walked toward him in a more confident manner, they were not even trying to protect themselves. John kept his eyes squarely on the cowboy and with his left hand; punched the 400 pound bouncer in the face. The 400 pound bouncer reeled and instantly put both of his hands up to his mouth and doubled over at the same time. John never took his eyes off of the cowboy. The cowboy did not have the same fighter's discipline. He took his eyes off of his opponent to see if his friend was all right. As he turned to see about his fellow bouncer, John reached back with his right hand and his body moved like a major league pitcher throwing a fast ball, at the same time the cowboy turned to face Johnathan Spectrum. John's right fist was waiting for him. The cowboys chin and John fist were both in motion and were simultaneously moving toward one another. John never took his eyes of his opponent he saw the fire go out of the man eyes. His fist struck the man squarely on the chin. His faced rippled in shock waves under the skin. His mouth exploded with blood, teeth, and spit as John punch through him and not at him. The cowboy hit the ground like the gunman did, like a boneless fish. Then the 400 pounder recovered from the initial punch, and shook it off. The 400 pound man was strong and there was no doubt about it as he threw haymaker after haymaker. He was big and slow, and John was the heavy weight champion of the world. John could hear the police sirens getting louder and louder. He thought to himself 'I ain't got time for this'. The big man swung at John, and John side stepped the swing and the big man tried to over compensate his haymaker punch and threw himself off balance. John completed the side step and while the big man was off balance. John kicked him in this ass and allowed his 400 pounds of weight and inertia to take him down to the floor; that dude fell like a rock, John could hear his impact with the floor as he ran out the front door.

******

The two computer Icons Doctor Taylor, and Colonel Sawyer looked at the images as they played out in Johnathan Spectrums mind. The Colonel Sawyer said; "That was a mere bar fight, any man could have handled that situation. Doctor Taylor said; "Yes, colonel you are the expert on tactics and strategy lets reprogram a more challenging scenario". The

Colonel said; "the movie industry for this time period is incredible. It gives of endless combat scenarios". The doctor reverted; "Yes the familiar images and the computer images are conveniently placed in pixels. We can program Mr. Spectrum on the subconscious level with subliminal information." "The last scenario we successful downloaded the instructions on how to use the apparatus; and how to use his empathic abilities." Mr. Spectrum does not know how strong his empathic ability is; he can read, others feelings and he can also project his feelings on to others as well." The Colonel said; "impressive, let's try something different. In the next programming he is to receive." "I will introduce him to a very creative scenario". The Doctor raised an eyebrow and was curious what his fellow artificial intelligence had in mind." Johnathan Spectrum ran through the front door of the bar. He ran right out of a strip club into a grave yard. John did not notice but he was transported back to a different time. He looked around himself and tried to get a hold of his bearings. As he looked around he was bare foot in the cold mud, he was wearing an old shirt and pair of pants. He looked long and hard at the trees they were willow trees. He thought out loud; "I am down south; "Oh shit, I am a slave." He was immediately jarred back into reality as he heard screaming. It was a dramatic scene unfolding in front of him, men on horseback with torches in their hands wearing white sheets and white hoods. They were shooting at the raggedy group of huts. They were throwing their torches into the dilapidated buildings and shooting the people as they ran out. John broke into an all-out sprint at the raiders. As he got closer he noticed that they were shooting anyone that ran out to the dilapidated houses women, children, alike. John felt pure rage as he ran into the middle of the raiders. John ran across the grave yard with reckless abandon. He reached the woodened fence and then he ran up the fence. This was a true testament to his physical prowess. He hit the fence in a dead run. His feet hit every slate on the wooden fence and in an instant he was at the top of the fence and launched his-self full body onto the closest raider. John landed on the raider full bodied, he hit him side ways and wrapped his legs around the raider so he would not fall off the horse. John grabbed the hand that had the reigns and reached over the raider's right shoulder and broke his neck so quickly that he could not call for help. In the confusion one of the fellow raiders shouted an alarm to the fellow raiders. John was still on the horse with the dead raider. He reached down to the dead man limp arm and seized his forty-five out to his hands. The raiders turned their horses and orientated their bodies to get a shot at John. John did the same. The horse was jittery from the burning buildings and the bullets flying around. John who still had a hold of the horses reigns grabbed the saddle horn with that hand, and shifted his buttocks on to the back of the horse. The raiders took a few shots at him and missed. John took that old forty-five and pulled back the hammer and shot the raider who sounded the alarm right between the eyes. The raiders were hesitant, and John did not know why. He decided to capitalize on this hesitation and shot another man in the face that called him a nigger and shot the horse out from under one of the raiders that tried to charge him and pull him away from his human shield.

The blacks who were victims of the raid started throwing stones and trying to hit the raiders with farm tools. They were emboldened by John's brazen attack. It occurred to John that they did not know the man that he shared the saddle with was dead. They shifted their attention from him to the poorly armed blacks with farm tools and started shooting at them and killing them. Johnathan full of rage said; "Stop or I will kill this confederate coward." "He used a load commanding voice. He cocked the hammer of the forty-five and prayed to God that he had at least one bullet left. The night raiders stopped and John screamed get the hell out of here! One of the raiders said; "We are not leaving with out our colonel." John did not think twice about the colonel remark. John then said; "Leave and I will let your precious Colonel live." John felt a pang of guilt because he knew he killed the man whom he was sharing this horse with. He put it out of his mind, John said; "leave"! He felt a strong release of energy that he could not explain. The night raiders and even the blacks turn around and abruptly walked away. John thought long and hard as to what to do. He felt if he left the colonels body for the raiders to find they would come back and take revenge on the blacks in this village. When the raiders rode away John seized the opportunity and laid the colonel's body over the horses back. Still in the saddle John reached down to grab a shovel that was propped up against one of the fence's post; that was being used as a weapon by one of the poor black people. John turned the horse away from the burning huts and the light of the flames. He rode out for an hour due west dismounted and apologized the beautiful black steed before he shot it. He was wondering what his task was here and he unhooded the colonel. John was shocked to speechlessness. Colonel Sawyer was more than a solider he was a night raider preying on recently freed blacks. John looked at the colonel's face and said; "I'd be damned." "I thought you were man of ignorant pride colonel." "I see you are more an animal than your horse was." Johnathan Spectrum was going to try and be respectful to this old 'soldier's body; but he felt too much rage for that. He buried the colonel in a deep grave. The ground was soft and muddy. He had to use the rope on the horse's saddle to pull himself out of the ten foot grave that he dug. He kicked the colonel into the grave, and said; "May God forgive you, because I won't." The Colonel landed in the grave face first, with his body turned in an awkward angle. Then John shoved that most brilliant black steed into the hole. He had to use his shoulder and push the horse into the grave while also using his strong leg muscles. He grunted and strained but the task was done. He felt more guilt for the dead horse than the dead confederate colonel. The beautiful black steed was pushed in the grave on top of the colonel. Before he buried the colonel, John took the painstaking time to look for clues of the colonel's whereabouts by policing the area for dropped items. John looked around for anything that my give away the colonels grave; as far he knew there was not anything. He looked around the forest and thought how breathtakingly beautiful this southern forest was. John took a small moment to look at the rising sun as he set himself to the task of burying this confederate. When he was nearly finished he took care to throw in that old forty-five and the shovel and pushed the rest of the dirt over the grave with his hands. John looked down at his hands and feet and thought how filthy he was. He got up and was going to put as much space between him and the colonel's body as possible; as he stood up and turned around, he reappeared in the chamber with the two A.I. Icons, Doctor Taylor and a homicidal looking Colonel Sawyer, looking at him. The portal of the chamber opened and John stepped out. He meets the colonel's gaze with his own, neither man backed away from the other, the doctor interrupted by clearing her throat. The two men still made eye contact and Doctor Taylor ask John if he was hungry and that they were done with his programming for today. John said; thank you doctor I could use refreshment. John turned his back on the colonel and that seemed to be more perturbing to him, because of John showing him his back. The Colonel's Icon disappeared and Doctor Taylor's Icon rushed up to join John as he walked to the open door in which they came in. Doctor Taylor was very cordial as she walked John around the pod. She went into great detail how the pod was a spaceship that was a kilometer long and had and radius of a circumspherse of a kilometer. Its physical shell was spherical, but due to the pod's extra-dementnial technology the inside of the pod was as large as the earth's moon. Johnathan Spectrum spent the majority of his time on the pod with Doctor Taylor. He did not care for Colonel Sawyer too much at all. The final hours in the pod were upon them. This programming session was going to be John dealing with and directly talking to the colonel. This was an attempt to give John a working knowledge of the Sentries and how they operate and give the A.I. Icon and

John some understanding of how they could work together under stress. John walked into the room that housed the capsule in which he was going to be programmed in. He would be programmed with another scenario, giving him command words, and showing him how to interact with the sentries. After John entered the capsule he laid back and rested and the capsule tilted at a 45° angle. The programming started a little different. John watched as the roof opened above the capsule, and then capsule launched into space. He felt the inertia on his body and the G-forces as he accelerated out of the pod into open space. The capsule tumbled end over end as it hit the atmosphere of a strange green planet. When the capsule hit the strange planet's atmosphere the centripetal forces in the capsule was nearly unbearable. The capsule hit something and tumbled faster. When John looked out of the capsule he noticed he hit the ground and was bouncing along and then he hit the green dirt, and tumbled until his momentum stop. John was so dizzy that he could not see straight. He was still tumbling in his head even though the capsule had now come to a rest on the strange planet's surface. John put both of his hands on his head as if the try and physically stop the spinning sensation in his mind. He slowly moved to get out of the capsule. The capsule open by the urging of his will. John's legs felt rubbery and he could barely stand. Then he heard it. It was shriek that sounded like a cross of human and eagle. He heard it again and it was louder. That unusual noise snapped him back into equilibrium; as John regained his bearings, he looks out on to the alien planet's landscape. The strange planet had a sun that looked smaller than his native sun. The landscape was semi-desert but the rocks had and unusually green film on them. The planet looked like earth but the colors and smells were different, he turned his body to get the whole panoramic view of the world. He looked at the mountain range that was some ways off in the distance and thought the mountains looked strangely familiar. He stared in amazement and he was shocked to recognize them as Egyptian pyramids. He was doubly shocked to feel and overwhelming sense of rage and malice. He had a split second to none as he saw a flash out of his peripheral vision. He instantly ducked and rolled out of the way. He was in a state of bewilderment, shock and awe all at the same time. He recognized the creature from history class, it was a man with an eagle head, it was astonishing, it had large bulbous eyes, and a sharp beck. The crown of its head was covered in feathers down to its shoulders. It had and Egyptian curve long sword. It was bare chest and wore the traditional man's garment wrap around its waist, and open sandals. He was a true representation of the ancient hieroglyphs. The half-eagle, half-man that every scholar studying Egyptology thought were just paintings and mythos. It swung its curved sword in an overhand chop barely missing John. Who so wisely decided to stand in another place? John was completely caught off guard. He has never seen a living contradiction, half-man half-eagle before. The large curve sword hit the hard and rocky desert soil and made a loud metallic clang. The half-man eagle looked at John as John looked at it. It looked at him like a bird of prey looks at a potential kill. It turned its whole head and gave him a long look with its unblinking eagle eyes. Then it blinked and in a flash it brought up the curved sword and slashed up. It moved with very fast non-human reflexes. Then it watches John uses his lightning fast human reflexes and dodge another killer blow. The half-eagle man stops and begins to circle John and John as if on cue began to circle it, neither opponent taking its eyes of one another. Now the half eagle half man put both of his human hands on the curve long sword. It was pointed at John's torso level. John wanted to fight back, he willed himself an Egyptian curved sword; and like that, it appeared in front of John. John reached out quickly to grab the sword. The half eagle half man turned its large eagle head and saw the curved sword teleport into John's grasp. It hesitated because it did not see anything so curious before. It looked at John again, cocking it head slightly right and blinking several times. John was now armed and could now defend himself. He felt a lot better about the situation. John stood there with the curved sword waiting for the half-man half-eagle to attack him. John felt the strangest of sensations that the thing was trying to read his mind, and John refused entry by his whim alone. The half-eagle man stopped moving. Then he attacked, it was the most vigorous and vicious sword volley that John has ever experienced. The half-eagle half-man moved like the trained killer that he was. John was able to keep up with every thrust and slash with a parry or dodge. The half-eagle man was quick and deadly. He would leave large rents in the ground where he would try a cleave John in half and miss. John would always move in a nick of time. He actually felt his arm ach from moving and parrying the half-eagle man's curved sword. John thought that he was not going to last for long fighting this creature in what he believed at its weapon specialty. He decided in a split second to change the tone of the argument. Every time the half-eagle man came in for the killer blow. After his incredibly fast sword slashes and thrust the half Eagle-half man ended the sequence with an overhand chop trying to cut John in two. John then saw how slowly he pulled his curved sword out of the ground. When the sword sequence came as expected the half-eagle man did not see it coming; John willed himself to teleport from in front of the humanoids 'great cleaving' motion to the rear of the half eagle man's sword arm. The half-eagle man's torso was hyper-extended as he went for the killing blow and missed. John had a split second to react; he looked at the half eagle man's shoulder blade and its neck. He decided to hit him in the shoulder blade. The half-eagle man shirked in pain; as the curved sword cut through his shoulder blade striking the bone. The half-eagle man turned so quickly the curved sword was knocked out of Johns hands because it was obviously stuck in the creature's bone. The half eagle man pulled the curved sword out of his shoulder blade. John standing there bare handed, was not going to wait for an invitation. He launched into a series of punch combinations. He hit the half-eagle man's beck with his bare hands and swooned in pain. The half-eagle half man was stun; to say the least. John thought to himself that he would not make that mistake twice. With his left hand he completed his punch combination with a strike in the half-eagle man bulbous eye. John struck the half-eagle man's eye and it shrieked and flushed in pain. John had to pull his hand free from the half-eagle half man's eye because the punch to the eye caused an involuntary eye closer; and the eye lid closed on John hands. John thought to himself, every giant has a weakness; and threw punch after unmerciful punch into the poor creature's eyes. He punched the creature into unconsciousness. John stopped punching, and said; "Well, that wasn't so bad." He heard an unusually chirping noise. It sounded liked an electronic bird chirp. He rolled the half-man-half-eagle creature over. He looked down to investigate where the noise was coming from. At the same time he found the source of the sound he heard what sounded like a thousand eagle cries. John looked down at the half-eagle, half-man creature and immediately thought "distress call"! John moved away from the creature's body just to make sure it was not a suicide weapon as well. He looked over the green sandy desert and saw dust trails coming his way. In panic he thought that he had no other choice, but to try and escape. He looked at the uncountable dust trails and back to the pod. John force himself to calm down and assess his situation. He said; "wait a minute"; he put his hand out and willed a pair of binoculars into his extended hand and they appeared. He looked through the binoculars and thought to himself that he needed a lot of fire power, and he had to kill as many of those things that he could. The thought heavy machine gun, and mini-gun came to mind. The more he thought about it, he noticed those creatures were wearing armor and wielded hand pole axes as well as curved swords on their sides. "Wow" he thought; "I never, thought in a million years that I had to contemplate how quickly and efficiently to kill another living creature". He put it out of his mind. He selected the mini gun with armor piercing rounds after he teleported the binoculars away. The eagle cry's got louder and louder, and John could now see the big brown parts of their eyes as they ran toward him. When he willed himself the mini-gun; the mini gun appeared in front of him. He reached out and took the mini gun before it dropped to the ground. John almost dropped it anyway because he was unprepared for the weapons weight. The ammunition was teleported down with the gun. John quickly set the gun down and put the ammo pack on his back. The half eagles were close enough to throw their pole axes at John. He quickly loaded the ammunition and picked the gun up to waist level. John pressed the on button and let the barrels get up to speed. He was suddenly put off balance because he had to dodge a pole-axed thrown at his head. He regained his balance the gun was heavy, even to him. He picked it up and pulled the trigger and wasted the creature that that tried to take his head. John fired and fired the whirl of the six barrels and the burp of the bullets leaving the barrel was deafening. John watched in horror as these half eagles just ran into the line of fire. He watched as limbs blew off, and chests exploded. He could not believe that he was capable of such an atrocity. He wanted to stop but knew that if he did he was going to die and he knew that they were not going to show him the same compassion. This enemy has no fear of death, they were truly dangerous. In the corner of his eye John saw a flash. He was all wet and when he recovered from the initial shock. He was covered in blood; one of the half-eagle men out flanked him. John heard firing, but it was not his firing. He put one hand on his head and shook off the confusion the sentries that Colonel Sawyer were controlling finally made an appearance. The sentries had one distinct shape they were oval like eggs and had a cluster of spheres rotating around their base. They were of varies sizes large as small automobiles and as small as microwaves. They were unpainted and were of a metal that could not be described by earth's standards. The sentries had human made weapons. The larger sentries had large guns 25 mm cannons, grenade launchers and heavy machine guns. The smaller ones had smaller weapons, sub-machine guns, rifles. John stood there and watched the massacre as it unfolded. He held the mini gun at his waist level as he watched the sentry drones attack the hoard of humanoids. He felt no need to fire his gun the creatures were being wiped out. He watched with a numb feeling and thought to himself I cannot do this to fellow humans. Johnathan willed the mini gun away and the curved sword that he dropped by his side and forgot about. He willed himself back to the pod and he was instantly teleported back to the capsule. He sat down by the pod trying to figure out what he was going to do next. The simulation ended and he was suddenly backed in the pod looking at the two computers Icons Doctor Taylor and Colonel Sawyer. They waited to speak before the pod open. The colonel spoke first "He said, "The first time out, even the best bird dogs are shaky". John looked at him and said, "I ain't going to kill anybody." Colonel Sawyer said, "John those things are living and breathing creatures yes, but they were created in a laboratory." John looked at him and said, "I was supposed to drive away another fe-loon." "I was not supposed to kill anything." Colonel Sawyer said; "Yes, but you have to protect yourself and take away its superior protections". You have to make the fe-loon abandon its human experimentations." The humans that are guarding its power grid and palace are augmented." "They are augmented with artificial genes and fe-loon technology." "John looked at him, and said; "How is that my problem, take me home." This fe-loon is going to do to this planet what the others did on earth"; Colonel Sawyer said. John looked and said; "What did they do on earth." "The human trafficking that your planet has experienced past and present came from this particular fe-loon". If allow to continue the humans that are being experimented on will be bred and sold to other fe-loons and other alien races." "You are requested to drive off the fe-loon think long and hard how many innocent children you will save from force labor and experimentation." The word 'children', caught John off guard. He never thought about the little children on the planet at all. Colonel Sawyer continued; "Where do you think you humans have got gold lust, and land ownership from"? "Think about that one; we are all human; but there are does among us who think that we are a master race." John looked up at the colonel, and the colonel's computer Icon turned away as if it was embarrassed. Doctor Taylor interrupted the exchange. I noticed that your heart rate and blood pressure are elevated. John slowly looked at the doctor. The Doctor said in a soothing voice; "Mr. Spectrum as soon as you complete this request we could teleport you home and you could resume your life of leisure. John was startled back to reality. He said; "how long have I been gone", "two Earth days the doctor said. We will be in orbit of the furthest satellite and we will stay there until the mission is complete." The Colonel said; "you will be launched onto the night side of the planet the fe-loon is residing in the southern pole of the planet. We will have two objectives shut down the power grid. The fe-loon has enough power to teleport a large army to Earth." The power grid is on the planet equators and is guarded by those half-man half eagle creatures that you were fighting. They are ten times faster and smarter than the simulation and they have limited telepathy. You have nothing to worry about they can't read your mind". That is the only advantage you have over them." "They are not human "They are engineered to kill and will not hesitate to do so." John looked tired and the doctor suggested that he rest before he starts his mission.

The capsule or spaceship which ever translation you prefer moved across space and time; and materialized in the designated teleportation point. John slept for a total of two hours and tried his best to relax; but he could not. He ate, tried to force himself to sleep and laid in his bed that the fe-loon created for him. He could not shake how he had made the wrong decision. He thought about it long and about the people who were en-slaved by a fe-loon. I was not supposed to kill but drive off. He hated the fact that he could kill his fellow humans but not the alien. He felt queasy and noticed that he was sweating. He has not felt like this since his first game as a rookie. Before he could continue to brood, he was summoned to the pod and the preparation area for his mission. He took off his pajamas and got into the shower. The capsule was a marvel of engineering as he washed himself the water came out in a consistent mist that saturated his body and in an instant he felt the water teleported off of his skin. He was dry and clean in least than 30 seconds. As he got ready he thought he would prefer a long hot shower versus the short efficient one. He left his living quarters as he step through the passage way he was immediately teleported to the preparation area. The teleportation process lasted less than a second. As he took his first step into the passage way, he was immediately teleported and re-materialized before his second step hit the ground. He was now in a room that he never seen before. The view was incredible. The colonel and doctor computer Icons were standing in front of him but he could not help to notice the vast array of weapons. He also could not help to notice the view of the planet behind the arsenal. The planet was a swirling mast of gases and it had active volcanoes erupting on its surface that can be seen this high in orbit. It looked as if that there was no wall or protection from the harshness of space. The Colonel cleared his throat and interrupted John's star gazing. The Colonel said; "Mr. Spectrum we are at our destination. I would like to go over the strategy before you disembark." John said; "O.K. did the situation change or something?" Yes; it did the colonel said. The humans are staging an uprising and the mission just got complicated. John stood there intent on listening. The human apparently are refusing to be slaves and are tired of being experimented on. The security at the fe-loons lair has increased 100-fold. He has an army of one million surgically altered and engineered soldiers." The colonel looked concerned, "The fe-loon has started a systematic extermination of the human population. John's heart just went to his stomach. John's said;

"Colonel how the hell am I going to drive off the fe-loon. The colonel shrugged and said, "I don't know, but we have to do something." The doctor said; "I noticed an increase in your heartbeat and an elevated blood pressure." John looked and the doctor and did not say nothing. John said; "Let's get this thing started, the quicker I stop this, the quicker I can get home." The colonel nodded his agreement. The doctor directed him to the pod and to the portable apparatus that he wore. The doctor helps him where she could but he figured out how to do it before. The doctor checked him over and said that; "We have a computer chip to give you." John said; "Why?" This computer chip will give you the ability to down load and use fe-loon technology. The computer chip was thin like a spider web and was so small it could not be seen with the naked eye. John thought about how useful it would be to download and use alien technology. He nodded in agreement; and the computer chip was teleported onto his brain stem. John did not feel the computer chip fusing with his brain matter and carried on with his conversation. He reviewed their language and universal translator itself in thirty seconds after receiving the computer chip. These human didn't speak any known language from my planet, he thought, they have developed their own languages and cultures. This chip also gives you a working knowledge of every last one of your weapons and vehicles assembled for your use. John looked up at that as his started put the pieces of the apparatus on. John said, "What are my assets, Colonel?" The Colonel said "Every weapon that human beings have ever created." John said, "Incredulously <u>every</u> weapon?" The Colonel looked back at him stoned faced and said; "<u>every</u> weapon!" John looks off into space, and thought about what that meant. Jonathan boarded the pod; and was instantly teleported to the fe-loon planet that was called a satellite. When John left the pod, the pod itself teleported back to the capsule. John began to walk away from the site in which he materialized. As he walked into the night it began to dawn on him that he was on another planet. The star constellations were incredible, so he walked slowly, as to take in the sights of this strange planet. The little animals that scurried about, and ran through the forest were so alien that John began to walk very slowly with wonderment in his eyes. While John walked he heard the colonel's distinct voice on his com-link. "John," the colonel said; "You don't have time to sight see. Teleport to the fe-loons palace and commence your attack. John said; "just like that?" The colonel retorted and said; "Yeah, just like that!" As John walked along he thought about his approach and what he had to do he made a plan in his head and went about implementing it. He recalled the palace and the grounds around the palace with uncanny detail. He looked around one last time at the beautiful night side of this new planet. Then he willed himself to teleport a mile and half from the fe-loons palace. As John step along into the alien planets night, he was actually still wonderstruck at the new and unusual sights he has seen. He walked along and was in a daze as he sight saw, this planet that was not earth. His daze did not last long, as he heard the incomprehensible conversation spoken at a distance. He could hear laughing and talking but could not make out anything else. He knew better than to walk up on to the unknown persons, so he crotched down and approached as slowly and as quickly as possible. He walks on and could make out a large fire and could make out those distinct shapes of the half-eagle half-man humanoids that he fought in the training simulator. His stomach almost turned, when he saw the most horrific sight in his life. Humans were hung upside down and were being bled and slaughter like cattle. John nearly wretched as the wind shifted and he could smell the cooking human flesh. A shade of rage flashed over Johnathan's face and said; "I got something that you can eat on"! He moved backed to a more concealable position and he thought about it and then he teleported a .50 caliber sniper rifle into his hands. John was enraged by the spectacle in which he saw. He waited and watched as he pick out what he thought was the leader. To his surprise it was not the largest humanoid. The smallest humanoid gave John the distinct impression that he was the smartest and was calling the shots. John was programmed with the working knowledge of all the weapons in the arsenal. This was another planet so the gravity is different and then the wind currents were different also. John thought to himself; "Breathe calm down, breathe," and he slowly pulled the trigger. The rifle firing surprised him as he concentrated on keeping the rifle level and straight. As he concentrated on the sights of his rifle he saw the tell-tale signs of the humanoids chest cavity exploding. John teleported himself 40 yards behind the camp site as the other humanoids turned the heads and their large eyes to the area in which the report of the rifle came. John was teleported to another position by now. The large humanoid that was butchering humans was next, and John had murder in his eyes. He concentrated again on the sights of his weapon. He slowly squeezed the trigger as he watched the humanoids head explode before he completely pulled the trigger back. The humanoids were not very smart but they were highly sensitive to noise and vibration. They turned to the noisy report of the rifle, and John was gone again; he rematerialized three and quarter miles away. He heard the bird like scream that the humanoids made when they were attacking. In real life it is louder and more menacing than the training simulator. John fired and fired until his magazine was low. He took great care into teleporting away from his firing positions. Then the humanoids got tired of dying and the laid down prone and into positions where they got 360° scan of their area. The camp itself was large, and it probably had one 150 to 200 of those half-human half-eagle things in it. As John watches his sights looking for targets of opportunity he caught movement out to the corner of his eye. The humanoids, had other humans and augmented animals, to aid in their search of him. John teleported away not wanting to be captured and he was shocked to find that he could not teleport away. He immediately opens a channel to the colonel.

John said; "Colonel, I cannot teleport away from this search party, am I doing something "wrong?" The colonel said; "You should have never engaged that camp of humanoids, now the whole vicinity knows that you are out there." Johnathan, the humanoids can communicate telepathically. They know you are a teleporter and they have a teleport detector/suppressor." John said; "What"? The colonel repeated; "They have, with them a teleport detector/suppressor." They can find you and prevent you from teleporting." John thought long and hard about his situation. It was three hundred of them and 1 of me. That's not good odds John thought. John said; out loud, "I got one chance, and only one chance." He looks for where that so-called teleport detector/suppressor device maybe located. He looked and it was obvious it was the only technologically advanced piece of equipment on the battle field. John checked his magazine and he three bullets left. "Colonel"! John said; "I have located to device any suggestion on how to deal with it." The Colonel said; "The device emits, an electromagnetic pulse, you cannot stand aloft and shoot at it." You have to get in close beyond the electromagnetic field and do it damage." John said; "How do I do that?" The colonel said; "I don't know but if you want to survive you will do something." John sarcastically responded; "Yeah, right." John looked around and he was running out of options. They were closing on his position fast. John slapped the magazine back into his rifle and shot and killed the humanoid closets to him. He ran as fast as he could to get to the humanoids curved sword. When he shot the humanoid he got up and slung the rifle across his back, he heard the half-eagle man scream that the humanoids used to raise the alarm. John sprinted to the humanoids body and picked up his curved sword. When the humanoid's body fell the other humanoids were drawn to the movement. The humanoids began to screech in rage as they saw Johnathan Spectrum running for the humanoids body. They instantly started to run at him. While John slung the rifle across his back and ran for the curved sword he did so in one fluid motion. When he made to the humanoids body he was met there by another humanoid. John duck under a huge swipe of the humanoids sword. He tucked and rolled under the blow and caught the sword by its pummel scrapping his knuckles in the process. Ignoring the minor pain, John grabbed the sword and landed on his feet after the roll's momentum slowed. He turned to face the humanoid, that creature was huge it was full of muscle and it is an augmented creation. John knew better than to tangle with this thing too long because he can see the other humanoids advancing on his position fast. The humanoid raised his curved sword in such a matter that John knew that he did not move; he was going to be cleaved in half! John moved while the death blow was coming down. He then noticed that he was incredibly strong and slow! John was completely out of his way before he had the sword completely committed to its down swing. John seized the opportunity and reversed the curved sword in his hand and struck the humanoid across his Achilles heel. The humanoid screeched in pain as it reared back, John struck it in the side of its neck. The blood was so thick that it was purple. John saw a flash of movement out the corner of his eye and he moved in the nick of time. Another humanoid had advanced on to his position. John looked at his current position and thought it was a no win situation. He had to move or he was going to be surrounded. John ducked at another swipe of the curved sword. He scrambled behind the humanoid on all fours, and then shoulder blocked him in the back toppling him over. These things are really slow, he thought. I can run rings around them. So that's what he did, when you are in doubt, go back to what you know. Johnathan Spectrum is a professional running back. He took off, he ran ducked weaved and bobbed, he ran in circles he change his speed and directions spontaneously. He ran for a while a good two and half minutes and he thought it was odd that he was not tired yet. He slowly and deliberately worked his way to the teleport suppressor/detection device. He was running under sword slashes and chops with relative ease. The years of beginning a pro running back has trained him well. Dodging sword slashes and thrusts was not what he originally dreamt of during his pee-wee football days. John ducked, bobbed and weaved his way through murder and mayhem. He finally made it to the transporter suppressor/detector. The six humanoids that were guarding it came out to meet him with swords in hand. John thought to himself de ja vú as he sped toward the six humanoids as if he was running toward the defensive line of an arrival football team. He came at them head on and as they brought their swords up into overheard chops. He noticed these humanoids were big strong and fast; but they were not very disciplined soldiers. They ran into and tripped over one another in their zeal to try and kill Johnathan Spectrum first. The humanoids created a massive tangle of muscle, sword swipes and confusion. John instinctively launches himself over the tangle of humanoids. They lost him for a second as the humanoids had to rotate their skulls and twist their necks to keep with Johns movements. By the time that the humanoids turned and scanned the area for John, he was up and running at full speed toward the teleporter suppressor/detection device. John made it the device and heard a different type of screech from the humanoids it sounded like fear. The colonel contacted John through 'his communication link. The colonel said that; "the device has an electromagnetic pulse generator, and it had to be destroyed." John said; "How", nearly out of breathe from his run. The colonel said; "at the very top of the device there is a red dome emitting and pulsing light, you have to break that dome and your teleporter will work." The colonel said; "by the way, you cannot use anything with a high velocity, because the magnetic field will repulse the kinetic energy." John said; "so I need something slow and strong to hit it with. The colonel responded with; "Yes, sir." and before Johnathan can do anything else, he heard the large thumps of running feet and a lot of screeches! The humanoid that was on his trail since the camp was still dogging him and finally caught him. John saw the flash out of the corner of his eye and barely got out of the way. The humanoid thrust, slashed, and kicked at John. John suddenly had an idea he had to act quickly or he would be over whelmed in a big hurry. He launch into an attack of his own. He chopped and slashed and when the humanoid meet every strike with a parry and dodge. The humanoid kicked John full in the middle of his chest. John fell back and deliberately back pedaled into the teleportation suppressor/detector. John made a very risky calculation to drop his sword, as he put his back up against the device. The humanoid twist its head and watches John as he dropped his sword and raised his hand to futile attempt to protect himself from the killer blow. The humanoid took the bait and raised his curved sword to cleave John in two. John stood there trying to show he had fear in his eyes. When he the half-eagle half-man humanoid man chopped down with both of his hands; John leapt out of the way at the last possible moment; and with a very disappointing clank and hiss the device stopped working. John noticed that the light emitting-dome was not pulsating any more. It fell to the ground and sounded like an empty trash can that was thrown in the street by careless garbage men!

"John"! Colonel Sawyer said. John heard him and reacted with annoyance and at the same time astonishment, "How are you able to communicate with me?" "I am not wearing a headset or a radio." The colonel responded and said; "The sound of my computer generated voice is being directly teleported to your ear drums." John was now more intrigued, and wanted to ask more questions; but, before John could the Colonel cut him off. I cannot explain it now we got to keep moving. John started running at a nice steady pace. The years of athletic conditioning were paying off right now, John ran across the dusty semi-arid plain to the so-called palace of the fe-loon. The colonel piped up again. "John, we got to get to the power grid and cut the power". That apparatus that you destroyed had a processor to send a signal to the palace when it went offline." The half-man half-eagle sentries are all alerted of your presence and are coming for you." John thought "great." John spoke out loud for the colonel to hear him. Where is the power grid, and I will try and take it off line as quickly as possible". John felt un-ease in the colonel's computer Icon, as it hesitated." For an Icon that was a computer program, the colonel has a lot of human flaws and showed a lot of human inconsistencies,

John thought. John said it again, and the colonel's icon was angry when it responded, "I don't know". John was still running toward a palace that resembled a Mayan pyramid when he stopped running; sweat was beading on his forehead as he panted to regain his breathing control. John bent over and put his hands on his knees out of breath and said; "What?" the Colonel said; "we or I don't know." John said; "What"! The colonel said, "I don't know;" again just as forcefully. John said; "Colonel I assume, with the utmost confidence that you earned your rank and you did not send your soldier's into action without a plan". The colonel responded, "I have no information, about that palace you are going to have to play it by ear so to speak."

"O.K. what about any sentries that the fe-loon may have, defenses, you know the usual. The sentries are the humanoids you have been fighting and killing. The palace is defenseless only with that exception. You can walk in through the front of the pyramid or you can go in through the sewers that the fe-loon is using to dispose of the bio-engineered byproducts and waste. John brain just did a 'hic-up'; he said; "What?" "John," the colonel said; "the fe-loon is using the indigence people of this satellite to experiment with." John pace slowed into a jog as he moved toward the palace. "In my military experience, 'knocking on the front door', the way you put in your century, is not a good idea." I strongly suggest you go in through the sewers. I want to warn you that it is in your best interest to avoid traps, because, we have every reason to believe that the traps are engineered for the un-augmented human species of this planet. "O.K. where should I start;

John said;" thinking about as he spoke it out loud. The palace is sitting on a chasm. Inside that chasm you will find a slow moving stream. While following the stream itself you will find a large sewer pipe that flows away from the palace. I am sending you a 'thought....' "What," John said. I am teleporting the thought and memory of this place to your sub-conscious. "What"! "John I don't have time to explain this. Think about where you are and where you need to be, the thought is there." He said O.K. John thought about it and knew where he had to be. John willed himself there, and he teleported there in that instant, into a chasm that was several miles inside the surface of the planet. The planets night side was turning day, and the planets sun was being to show through the top of the chasm. John saw the natural fissure in the cavern wall where the small stream flowed from. It was not lit, so John had a Swat team issued semi-automatic shot gun teleported to him, it instantly appeared in front of him chest high and within arm reach. As the 50 caliber rifle disappeared; John casually reached out and took the shot gun out of mid-air as it appeared; cut on the small light, and racked a round into the chamber; he raised the shot gun up to his shoulder to look down the sights. He had to wander was that another thought process teleported into his mind, because that was too fluid, he thought. I am no dirty Harry I am freaking athlete. John pushed the thought out of his mind. As his entered the fissure he said, "Colonel, please explain to me what these human traps are and what they can do. "Well, the human traps are things made especially for humans. John moved down the fissure with a look of bemusement on his face. "I gather that part; please be more specific." "O.K." The Colonel said; giants, were wolfs, goblins, gremlins, unicorns; all these things are human specific. Now John was really surprised at his answer; and before he can respond. The colonel said; "John we are going to have a long talk about human history". "You have no idea how much advance alien life forms have manipulated and influence humans and human development". The slight smile of bemusement was no longer on his face. Now it was a look of skepticism, I just been transported to a planet you call a satellite, with no name and to a part of the galaxy or universe unknown to mankind. "I am smart but, not smart enough to know the difference. I have killed hybrid human beings that resembled Egyptian hieroglyphs of half-eagle half-man." "Colonel," try me!" The Colonel said; "O.K. you have a point". "Unicorns, giants, Pegasus, medusa, fairies; human beings have seen these things before." John stumbled inside the dark cavern; as he stepped, because of how surprised he was at the former statement. "Colonel you got to be joking." The colonel said; "No, I am not." "I am a computer Icon, lying and deception are beneath me". John digested what he said, John began to walk again, through the dark fissure; but this time began he watch his steps more carefully. Colonel, began again, "human beings have seen these things all of these fictional monsters before, these so-call legends are in most part base in facts, and are not a figment of someone's active imagination the fe-loons are only one race of non-humans who have, raped, murdered, kidnapped, and enslaved our race of man". John was astonished at the comment, as he moved further and further into the fissure he could see a sight glow; and hear a humming noise. John not knowing where to go; he moved toward the sound and light. John, said; "Colonel, I see light, and hear a slight humming noise". The colonel paused before answering. He said; "you are inside of the palace you are walking up to a waste disposal area be very careful". "Now, John prepare yourself for the horrors you may see". "Be careful"! John did not have time to think about the horrors that waited for him. When he heard the distinct shriek of the half eagle-half man humanoid, he raised his shot gun and made sure that the safety was off. The glow became brighter and brighter as he got closer and closer. He can now hear human suffering, screaming, and yelling. This human species spoke an entirely different language, but anger and fear is universal. John could tell by the tones of the different voices. John notice that the fissure's walls and ceilings were smoothed out and the area in which the waste disposal pipe was buried into the ground is where the medical waste and byproducts were thrown into the pipe. John felt that he had no other option but to run out and meet whatever dangers and horrors that was in the waste disposal area; so seeing that he wasn't not in navy seal or a ninja. John thought surprise was his best option. John stops at a place inside the fissure that would not expose him to light, or non-human eyes. He took in several breathes and then ran out with the shot gun up to his shoulder. What John saw made him swoon in disgust. The fear and horror that was supposed to greet him did not come; but anger did. In the middle of the room was of grinder and the human beings were being thrown in it alive! Females and males were literally thrown into a giant plexi- glass container; there were bodies in all states of injury; male, female, adult, and child, old, young. There were holes machined into the plexi glass container. The people inside the box were still alive, and were being crushed by the weight of the other humans that were thrown in top of them. Appalled and outraged John, moved the shot gun sights up to his point of view and shot the two humanoids that were doing the grinding. When he came around the corner into the light the initial shock of what he saw wore off; but the initial shock for the humanoids was short lived too.

John had to rapidly assess the situation. It was a real horror show; it was a waste disposal area on an industrial level. The waste of course was human bodies and human body byproducts. He saw the huge transparent cube packed to the rim with appeared to be live humans, and four humanoids in total, two that appear to be working and other two for security. Then John saw a crowd of patch worked humans standing in a formation of 4 by 4 totalling 16 people. These people had different body parts and were in different stages of decay. The two humanoids that were doing the grinding they were the closest to him and he being a prudent man thought he had to eliminate them first. The Colonel chimed in, "remember, short controlled burst, don't spray and pray." "Center Mass." John actually was grateful for the direction, because he was overwhelmed by the sight and sounds and horrific smells that that greeted him at the waste disposal area. He held his weapon up to his shoulder and looked through the sights. He pulled the trigger of the shot gun and watched as the chest exploded of the first humanoid unfortunate enough to be his immediate threat. The shock and surprise turn to anger for the humanoids as John killed the one humanoid that was grinding human flesh. The second grinder picks up the body of one of their victims and threw it at Johnathan, Johnathan ducked out of pure reflex. The half human, half eagle attacked; rushed John while John was in a crouching position. The humanoid was not fast enough. John shot him in the leg that was supporting to its body wait at the exact moment to begin to run flat out at him. The leg exploded from the magnum shot gun shell and it fracture and collapse in a bloody mess from its body weight. In John's peripheral vision he saw motion moving at him. At an impossible cycle of speed; but that object was not moving faster than his mind and reflexes. John saw an axe travelling end over end toward his face. His peripheral vision caught the movement, and John's will teleported him out of the way, a millisecond before the axe struck him. John adjusted to the new threat and didn't realize how loud and piercing that eagle shrieks were, until now, now that he was in an enclosed area. The second axe came flying by as John teleported back into the original spot he teleported from. The two humanoids were running flat out at him with the curved swords in hand. John raised the semi-automatic shot gun and shot them both in their bird faces. Blowing off the first attacker's beck and blowing out the second ones, right half of its bird brain. John looks over to the cube and was trying to figure out what he was going to do next. John said; "Colonel," what should I do next?" The Colonel said; "leave the waste disposal area immediately!" The fe-loon knows you are there it cannot read your thoughts, but it can read the thoughts of the others in the room. Get out of there, you are too exposed.

John said; "I cannot leave, there are human beings in that cube, help me get them out. The Colonel said; "John, get out of there before you are surrounded!" John said; "Surrounded by whom,"? Just then it hit him the incredible stench of rotten flesh. The sixteen patch worked humans were nearly on top of him. John reveled back because of the sight, and smells of the animated corpses. "Colonel", John said, as he ran back to give himself a reactionary gap. "Where should I go from here?" The Colonel said; "the door is directly behind the four animated corpses that stayed in their original position. Oh, I see it, John thought to himself this will be easy, I seen a lot of zombie flicks. John stopped running when he thought he got to a respectable distance and blew the head off of the first of the zombies. The zombie did not fall over dead to John's shock. John began to panic he did not know what to do; "Colonel." John called out with obvious, fear in his voice. The Colonel said; "What's wrong"! John said; "I shot one of the zombies and it did not die"! The Colonel said; "calm down". It is an animated lifeless corpse. It is being control by the fe-loon directly. You have to completely destroy the corpse; you just can't shoot it in the head. This is not the movies this as real life!" John felt surprised; by the last statement. "This is not the movies, this is real life." John stopped to think about how he can destroy a human body. There were probably a thousand answers to that question; but he settled on the first one that came to mind. John, teleported more shells into the magazine of his shot gun. Throw the shot gun over his back and tightened the sling so the shotgun would not bounce around. He then wills a sledge human into arms reach in front of him.

John reaches out and grabbed the sledge hammer. He was rapidly running out of reactionary space. The Twelve zombies were walking toward him at a brisk pace. There was no moaning and shuffle of feet on the ground. John took the sledge hammer and immediately teleported directly to the left flank of the formation and used that sledge hammer on knees and hips. John broke the legs of the first zombie, it collapse but still kept coming. Then the zombies shifted there direction and increased their velocity and speed. The zombies pivoted ninety degrees to their right which was John's left at the time as they turned to chase him. He teleported directly behind the formation and clip the legs of the nearest two from behind. The zombies began to react faster, John noticed that the zombie to John's immediate right reached out and tried to grab him; he took the sledge hammer and swung it with wicked and brutal efficiency. He broke the things elbows, right shoulders and left collar bone. John teleported in and out to the formation as it twisted and turned on to itself, the zombies where stumbling and running over themselves trying to kill Johnathan. Snapping, cracking, popping; that was the grotesque sounds of bones breaking and being force out to their natural positions; it took John twenty minutes and some considerable effort to break their bones and to make them immobile. That's when the four left their positions near the doorway. This group came running at him full speed. John was so out of breathe and his arms were sore from swinging that sledge hammer that he teleported the sledge hammer away; and went straight for the shot gun sling across his back. He removed the shot gun from his back; switch the shotgun from safe to fire and; Boom, Boom, Boom. He knee capped all four of them. John proceeded with the second part of the plan. He wills the shotgun away and teleported a flame thrower in to his hands, with fuel tank at his feet. John was thoroughly exhausted and hesitated a little as he put the tank on his back. The zombies were still trying to crawl toward him. It was amazing to see a mass of human parts, wiggling around like a swarm of maggots. John lit the pilot flame and aimed the flame thrower, with a long burst of flame followed by another and than another the animated corpses stopped moving and were utterly destroyed. John willed the flame thrower away and, got down on one knee to catch his breathe. "This little adventure is very, taxing I don't think I could finish." The Colonel responded; "Now; out of the room and I would send you some refreshments and some simulates if you want them. John moved from room to room and found an area that looks like a rain forest. That's when John started to fill real fatigue. The running and dodging attack after attack his starting to take its toll on him. He ran into a large room that appears to be an atrium with foliage indigenous to earth. "Colonel, I am alone and out of immediate danger". The colonel said; "stand by". Johnathan felt the sensation that something was teleported to him, but he could not see it. He began to feel the fatigue and pain go away. John said; "Colonel did you do something?" "Yes, I teleported stimulants and pain killers into blood stream; how do you feel?" "I feel fine;" John said. When Johnathan stopped speaking a square container was teleported to him also. It had what appeared to be vitamin infused water with chilled fruit in it. John ate and was very appreciative of his light lunch it did make him feel better. While he sat there, he started to think about his dilemma. He thought he may have bit off more than he could chew. He thought more and more about his agreement he made and was starting to regret it. John was suddenly broken from his contemplation by the all to familiar eagle shriek that proceeded attacks, he looked around the artificially garden; It was real plant life as far as he could tell he had the smell and the sounds of a rain forest, populated with earth's distinct wildlife. John looked at it and could not see the end of it from his point of view and decided to get out of this room. The tray with all of its remnants of food was teleported away. John let the professional running back in him come out. He took off for the door and as he made his way for the door the humanoid that was tracking him was right there on top of him. He ducked as the humanoid, slashed at him with its talons. John recoiled into the room and he zig zagged just in case the humanoids were following him. It was not chasing him; it stopped at the door and was accessing the situation. It turned its head as if a bird would; watching him with it bulbous eye. The humanoid was to not like the other half eagle and half man, this humanoid was female! She came after him with that distinctive eagle shriek! John did not takes long with his assessment either. She had well defined muscles and was moving a lot quicker than her male counter parts. John did not want to go backwards into the jungle; and thought about it he could dodge her with some tactics he learned on the grid iron. He ran at her as she ran at him. He ran at her flat out, head on with no deviation. She stopped her movement, with an abrupt halt, by slamming her lead foot down in the mud, and gave John that look that birds do when they are contemplating you. I guess she was not use to a person attacking her. John ran at her anyway, and when he was in arms reach, she slashed at him with her claws. John ducked under the first slash with no problem; the second slash came so fast it was incredible to comprehend. John being a professional running back got a small cut from her claws as she wasted time slashing with her second hand. She was off balanced and, he thought he could run by her and avoid a fight, but could not. She pressed her attack with hand speed that John had never experienced, in his years as a prize fighter. When he felt those talons dig into his chest, he knew then. Trying to run by her was a really bad idea. The female humanoid's fighting skill was incredible, as well as her hand speed. She slashed at him with over hand and wide angle arches with both her hands talon. John was able to parry and block or dodge the deadly strikes coming at him. She was not too much of a fighter she was going for the killer blow with every single strike. She had John on his heels, as John recoiled and step back from her killer blows. John felt that he had to change, 'the center of gravity,' so to speak; he had to start attacking her and put her on the defensive. Then he saw his opening and went for it. He jab at her, and struck her in the large eye that dominated nearly the whole side of her head. She involuntarily blinked from being struck on the eye ball. When her eye blinked closed, John struck her again, in the same spot with her eye lid down. She shrieked in pain, and turned her head to the right to look for him with the other eye. John saw that she had the same weakness that the male humanoids have. Those large bulbous eyes that help them with keen eagle vision are a liability in a close quarter fight. John just let all of his skill and training as a professional prize fighter show. He ducked, bobbed, and weaved as the humanoid, shriek from being hit by him. The female humanoid was stunned and partially blinded as he struck her, every time she forces one of her eyes open. John heard the shrieking of more of the humanoids from the opening doorway! "Damn," he thought; I really ain't got time for this shit! I got to put her lights out, and I don't want the bad Karma for killing a woman. Non-human or not, I got issues about killing a female." John teleported, in the instant when both her eyes were closed from the jabs he was giving to her large eyes. He appeared a millisecond later, behind her with a crow bar and struck on the base of her neck just under her skull. The female humanoid gave an involuntary shutter as her whole body want limp. She fell face first in the mud, as John could tell she was still breathing. He felt letter and look toward the door way. This was a group of humanoids, 4 total. They were wearing body armor. "Colonel," I got 4 humanoids, wearing what appears to her Egyptian armor." Should I be concerned?" John pivoted on his heels to run towards the rain forest, he was struck in the shoulder by a cross bow bolt. "Sun of a ..." the Colonel responded; "what's wrong"? "I was shot in the back by a cross bow"; John said; as he started running faster and in a zig zag pattern. He was reeling from the pain when the Colonel said; "to answer your first question, no, you should not be concerned". The fe-loon race doesn't have weapons, or the desire to create weapons. This fe-loon is using the weapons and armor available at this planets technology level. It is bronze Armor, nothing that you can't deal with. John said; "O.K. Colonel, I am bleeding really badly. The female humanoid did a number on my chest and the male humanoids behind me are armed with cross bows. I have been shot through my shoulder and I am beginning to fill fatigue from teleporting weapons, or the desire to create weapons. This fe-loon is using the weapons and Armor available at this planets technology level. It is bronze armor, nothing that you can't deal with. John said, "O.K." Colonel I am bleeding really bad the female humanoid did a number on my chest and the male humanoid behind me are armed with cross bows. I have been shot through my shoulder and I am beginning to feel fatigue from my blood loss. The Colonel said; "understood, please give me a second to create a solution to the formula to you have presented me with." It literally took one second John was in full stride, and running a zig zag pattern. He was no longer, fatigued, or in pain and the cross bow bolt stuck in his arm it was gone. The Colonel Teleported, the cross bow bolt out of his shoulder blade, and Johns cells were teleported out of his body, cloned and teleported back into his body. There was no longer any pain or a scar from either wound. John felt his strength come part and ran into the rain forest for cover. As he ran into the rain forest he could hear the other cross bow bolts striking the trees around him, as he turned to assess the situation. The humanoids began to fan out and enter the artificial rain forest area. John thought it would not be a good idea to teleport inside of a densely wooded area. John tried to account for the humanoids, and assess his tactical situation. He was no solider but he was a professional football player. In some respects the defense and attack manner were similar. He thought he counted twenty they were actually waiting for the ones whom fired their cross bows to reload. They were being to form up into a semi diagonal formation. They were arrayed and such away that they all had a clear line of sight with there crossbows. They could all cover one another and not be in a friendly fire situation. Well, John thought; "If they catch me and this rain forest I think I am going to loss my life here." I don't want to die here on another planet. John did not run out of the rain forest, he walks out, as he walks on he ran through his weapon options in his brain. He settled on the S.A.W. Squad automatic weapon with a box of belted armor piercing tracer rounds. The S.A.W. materialized in front of body at waist level and within arms-reach. He reached out and took the weapon and looked at the humanoids; they raised their crossbows and trained their mundane target sights on to him. They did not wait for an order or an invitation to fire. John saw the crossbow bolts flying at him. It was as if time completely stopped for everyone else but him. He saw the bolts coming at him, he blinked in and out of material existence, in a fracture of a millimeter here, and a half inch there to the left, right, forward, back. Not one cross bow bolt struck him or came near him; because he willed himself out of the paths of the oncoming missiles and teleported back into place as they past his current position. Every last projectile passed his current position. As he teleported back, he opened fire. "Don't spray and pray," he thought. There was too many of them he thought again; as his switch his weapon from safe to fire.

He held the S.A.W. at waist level, and pull and the trigger. The sound from the weapon was deafening, in such a confined space. He watches the tracers' direction of fire. Then he adjusted and walk the rounds back and forth over the formation. The rounds were striking the humanoids, so quickly that there were a few, who stood there not realizing that they were shot. The last pass John made was a figure eight; and got the few that did not know they were dead yet. John decided to stick with the S.A.W. and teleported a full box of ammo onto the gun. He charged the weapon and put a fresh round in the chamber. He went for the doorway, this time it was a task; because of the bodies and the blood that was all littering the immediate area and was directly behind the carnage. John had to scrap gore off the bottom of his shoes before he left the artificial rain forest room.

He ran down the hall way at a jog trying to conserve his energy. The hall way was well illuminated and I did not give the impression that this was in a pyramid, and a human slaughter house. The Colonel said; "John, you are almost there you have another large area to go through this might be the one!" John; said "the one?" Yes, the Colonel said the big one. Before John could ask, what is the big one? The Colonel, said; "The biggest fight you probably had in your life. You get through this you would probably be changed forever." John thought; "change forever," he sound like a Marine Corps commercial. "John kept his bemused thoughts to himself. He began to quicken his pace as he came to what appeared to be the end of the hallway. John, you are here, be careful"; the Colonel said. John walked into the entrance way and saw nothing that they gave him alarm. He walked in and as soon as the second foot was inside of the threshold; a wall appeared behind him hiding his exit. 'Wow' ! He thought that was too much; I should have seen that one coming. John walks further into the large open area, no windows, no doors he was wondering, how he was going to get out of there when. A man materialized in front of him. He was a well-muscled man, short in stature. He had a shaved head, and was wearing a uniform that John could not recognize nor identify; But the Samurai Sword in his hand was very distinct. "Colonel," John said; there as a small man in front of me with a Samurai Sword." The Colonel said; "He is imperial Japanese solider from the Great War that was before your life time and well after my own. I know of all the accumulated data that our fe-loon has collected about this mans people. He was chosen like you and I: because he had innate abilities born to him like you. "Really," John said, "What are they"? He was born with the ability to generate two times more testosterone than an average human male. He has been bio-engineered to use all of the testosterone his body produces and with hard wired reflexes were his adrenaline in constantly being produced and stored in his muscles. He is going to be the fastest and strongest fighter you will face. He is also a teleporter like you so be careful. John said; "I am the Heavy weight champion of the world." We'll see. John walks over toward him and the Japanese solider walks over toward him. John raised the S.A.W. and squeeze off a burst of rounds. The solider teleported in front of John at a ninety degree angle; when he materialized he was in full motion with his samurai sword. John had his own reflexes and they saved his life. He saw the motion in his full forward view and ducked while simultaneously raising the Squad Automatic Weapon. The Japanese Solider went straight for the killing blow. All of the humans and non-humans in this particular fe-loon's employ are killers. That Sword struck his weapon and made an incredible spark as that sword steal dug into the guns steel casing. John recoiled from the swords impact and was in a low crotch hiding behind the only protection he had. The Japanese solider tried to pull the sword from the gun casing where it cut through and was embedded. The Japanese solider was a professional solider he did not hesitate to teleport the sword away. While he simultaneously teleported a 9mm pistol inside his hands. John did the same and was barely saved again by his innate ability of not being able to be mind read. He teleported away the damaged S.A.W. and teleported in its place an S.W.A.T. team ballistic shield. It was black and large where John could hide his whole body behind it. This ballistic shield had a view port that had ballistic glass to protect the handler. The Japanese solider fired the 9mm pistol at the same moment the shield was teleported directly on to John's waiting arms. John recoiled as the ballistic shield caught the 9mm round fired into it. He watches as the ballistic glass crack and not shatter from being struck with pistol bullets. John had to think fast; this man came from a time when Kevlar was not invented yet, so he never encountered a full body S.W.A.T. team ballistic shield. He was no dummy; he still knows what armor is. John realized that he stop firing. John and the solider made the briefest eye contact before that went at it again for over an hour the two of attacked, and counter attacked, parried, dodged, lunged and feinted. Thy where both equally matched in some skills and ability; but those skills and abilities that one hand that the other did not was compensated for with other skills that one had and one did not have. John was starting to get tired he had to out think this guy and have several thought out and committed to before he can attack. This was Japanese solider, honor was his ideology. He would always come at me straight up. All those muscles mean he needs more oxygen than I do. John teleported stun gloves on to his hands and put his dukes up the Japanese solider willed his weapon away and went into a Karate stance. John did not charge him, he knew better. John walks toward him and the two combatants meet. The Japanese solider was incredibly fast. His hand speed was blinding. John never was struck so hard, and so quickly by an opponent. He teleported a large drum of riot control C.S. gas into the room and teleported it with its seal open. John fought him and match him strike for strike, counter move, with every move. He waited until the cloud of gas started to float over them. Then the solider who was breathing heavy and his pores were open from excreting himself; began to feel the sting of the chemical of the C.S. gas. John did not hesitate when he saw his nose running, and his eyes turning red. He went to work on the soldier's mid-section, by pounding his ribs with jabs and punches. He finally got the picture and teleported a gas mask on to his face. This was an old style gas mask that severely hindered a man's vision and his peripheral vision. The soldier was just as deadly and just as fast. John had to out think him. The solider got his bearings back and went into his fight routine. The CS gas was beginning to affect John also, he teleported a gas mask on to his face. John had a hard time ducking and dodging but he managed. The Japanese solider was a combat vet and did not fall for any of john's fighter's tricks. He kept himself well composed and waited patiently for his opportunity. It came; he hit John so hard; John doubled over in pain. John had to take a knee to recover from the strike. The Japanese solider went for the killer blow; He raised he hand into a karate chop aimed for Johns vertebrae while john was on one knee slightly turned with his back toward him. Johnathan Spectrum ran out of ideas and teleported the first thing that came to mind. He willed a door breaching ram used by SWAT teams. He gripped the ram by its handles and swung it into the mid-section of the solider. The ram and the soldier's body meet at the same time as he came down toward John with his killer karate chop. The ram was solid steel encased in rubber it blew all the air out of the soldier's lungs and knocked him off his feet on impact. Johnathan in one fluid motion teleported the ram away, sprang up to his feet and hit the solider with a punch that made him the heavy weight champion of the world. John Looks down at the solider laying on his stomach on the floor having involuntary muscle spasms as he lay unconscious. John said; "Colonel," I could use another on of those energy drinks. John teleported away the COST gas cloud, canister, his gas mask and the stun gloves; he bent over at the waist with both hands on his knees to try and catch his breath and slow down his breathing. The Colonel Teleported energy drink down to him. Cool to the touch but warm going down; an instant pick me up. John teleported flex cuffs and cuffed the Japanese solider. While John was cuffing him he had an opportunity to exam bend more closely. He was wearing a teleportation apparatus like John was. He looked like a throw back from that old movie Tora! Tora! "Colonel could you tell me who and what type of solider he is". The Colonel did not take long to respond. He said, "He is an Imperial Japanese solider; an officer born in 1928 and was pressed into to service for the fe-loon we are here to drive away from bus planet. Wow he and I were resent by extra territorial for the same reasons. They need a pone in there universal chess game. The Colonel said; "I would not have put it like that but kind of, yes". "Colonel I don't mean to be rude; but I can't keep this cat and mouse game up for too longer. I got a professional football and boxing career to get back to. How do I end this and go home. "Well, the fe-loon is behind that armored wall that you were standing in front of. How do I get to him and drive him off; "John said. The Colonel said; "I don't know, look through the inventory of your arsenal, I am quite sure you will think of something. John allow images of the human arsenal be teleported into his immediate view and he cycle through image after image. I decided on a low yield nuclear bomb; John teleported it to his immediate vicinity and set the timer for ten seconds. John said to himself; "let's see if I can win this thing with an old fashion Bluff." He stood there and waited; he began to sweat bullets. When the timer got down to three seconds, he watch the imperial Japanese solider materializes in front of him. John stops the timer at 1 second. John looked at the flex cuffs lying on the floor as he felt the sensation ease. He actually no longer could feel a presence in the room, that's when he knew. The Colonel said, "Congratulations, You drove it away, John good work!" John still felt uneasy. How much time do I have to get back to earth I got a fight coming up. It took up a couple of earth hours to get here, and you have been on this planet less than 2 earth hours. If took me what, and how long? John relaxes that teleportation technology that the fe-loon who recruits you is beyond human reason. John stood there completely stunned. He was brought out of his feeble minded thinking when he heard the shrieks of many half eagle-half man humanoids that appear to be converging on his present location. The room he was in was large like a cloned stadium. The doorway he walked through reappeared, as a cave entrance. The humanoids were of all different states of development from small, were large, small and young, like children young, male and female. "Colonel, I got a problem. I got a lot of pissed off humanoids running flat out at me. I don't have a clue! The Colonel said; "no problem". A hand cranked Gatling gun materialized in front of John. John cocked on eyebrow and ran over to the anachronism. He started turning the hard crank when they were and nearly too arms lengths away. Those things were really pissed off. They ran into his line off fire. They shot cross bow bolts, at him and threw every primitive missile that they had. John teleported in and out of material existence, with the Gatling gun, changing angles of attack and positions; John teleported full magazines into the gun as he went. He had to stop firing as the gun smoke obscured his vision and he was slipping from the old shells falling to the floor of the large room. John heard shrieks that were becoming quieter and quieter. As the smoke cleared John realized that when the carnage started the female humanoids pick up the small ones and B-lined for the nearest exit. John felt a little relieved, but saw how nasty a weapon that Gaiting gun was. He teleported him self to the door, because he did not want to step in Blood and brains that was all over the floor. As John walked thru the door he saw naked humans running and screaming every where. He also saw the drones moving about the hall way. They were broadcasting orders and instructions to the people in their dialog. John watch as a clutch of survivors was herd down the hallway to what he believes is the exit. John just was suddenly reminded of the waste disposal area. He ran down the metal hallway from whence he came, and saw that box of humans still in that grotesque state of being packed in. John teleported down a pneumatic jack hammer and broke the box open by its base. He watches in horror and relief he found a mechanism that opened that Plexiglas box. He opened the plexiglass and watched the human bodies pour out of it on to the floor. It was hard to believe that any one could live through that, but there were some survivors and John had a hard time separating them. John called for some drones for assistance. The drones scanned for life signs and found seven survivors two more that what John found. John could not walk away from the gruesome scene but at the same time he did not want to stay. It took some time for the humans to be evacuated from the pyramid. John was the only human that was not of there planet and was not enslaved and experimented on. The humans were in bondage so long those they only knew the humanoids. John had to send orders through the drones and the drones translated for him. He led them to a small valley that was near the pyramid that looks like their village, before the fe-loons and humanoids. Colonel I don't know what to do next the people are safe for the time being; what now? John; "standby". I am going to consult our fe-loon for an answer. John reluctantly said; "O.K." He looks at the pond, and he looked down at himself. Then he lifted up his right arm and smelled underneath his arm pit. He was offended by his own smell as he jerked his rose away from his arm pit. John looked at the pond again and looked around at the newly freed humans. He thought to himself there naked too. John took off his body armor and had clothes, he looked at the areas of his battle wounds and was impressed at how, regenerate cells were teleported into his body that accelerated his rate of healing nearly instantaneously. The humans watch as he got naked and walk into the cool waters of the pond. As he bathed the humans also began to follow his example and walked into the cool water of the pond. The feel of the mud and algae between their toes made a few of them laugh and smile. John did not realize as he watch the others clean himself three of the woman had waded over to him from behind; he turned around abruptly because he felt some ones presence behind him. He immediately relaxed as he saw three young petite women behind him. They all had long up kept hair. Their bodies were wet from the pond water. All three girls stood there with erect nipples waist deep in pond water John could not help himself as the women gingerly walk over toward him and began to touch his well muscle shoulders and arms.

John knew this was wrong, but he wanted it so much. The women surrounded him as he wrapped his left and right arm around the too tallest of the three and the small one wrap her hands around his torso. Hairy arm pits, bad breath, and unshaven vaginas this was so erotic. John could fill the girl on the right reach down and grab his hard penis. He looks her in the eyes as she began to stroke his manhood. Up and down, as the girl on the right started licking him like a cat would lick a kitten. The women started licking him. John had to look around; he was not the type that got busy in the public eye. But, he noticed that was how they clean themselves and one another. The humans were pouring water on to each other and then licking the area to be clean. He was suddenly pull out of his silent made contemplations as the small one in the front started licking the tip of his penis and started working her way down to his sack. The girl on the right was licking his armpit as the girl on his left licked his back and kept stroking his member. John felt greatly aroused and he grabbed the girl on her knees in front and gently by her hair and held her head in place and slowly pushed his penis inside of her mouth.

At first she seems like she did not understand; but she got the picture. John slowly pushed his penis further into her mouth as he gently held her head still by her hair. John started slowly thrusting and pumping her mouth as the other two girls licked him behind his ears and in his arm pits. They went up and down his body. John reached down picked the petite one up and gestured for the girl on his right to take her place and do what she was doing. John was so caught up in the moment that he starting licking them back. He licks her face, her ears and her hairy armpits. John and the three girls eventually made it to shore were they began to lick John's bottom half. The girl that was originally on his left; that was licking his back was licking him down below now. He bent over and arched his back for her as she gave him her best effort. John began to involuntarily vibrate, and explode from being sucked in the front and licked in the back. He watched as the short hair girl swallowed his semen; and look at him with eyes of admiration and appreciation. John crawled up on to the cool green grass as to three girls began to clean each other. It was amazing and incredibly unusual to see three hundred people, male, female, elderly and young clean themselves and one another and such a manner. John slowly drifted off to sleep as he thought to himself, 'Now I have seen it all.'

John, John, John! Wake up. John said; "how did you know I was sleep"? The Colonel said; "I could hear your snoring; you snore so loud that the sound did not have to be teleported to me I could just hear you". John kept his smart ass comment to his self. He said; "how long was I asleep"? "About 10-15 minutes; the Colonel said. We devised a plan you can teleport back to the pod, and return to the capsule as quickly as humanly possible. The men in your government are interested in hearing about your extra-terrestrial adventure. John grimaced. More bullshit, he thought please standby, I am moving as quickly as a tired human can move. John put on his gear and gave a longing look and an appreciative smile to the women who bathed him. He teleported back to the pod and the pod returned to the space capsule. John was back in Orbit with the fe-loon and the computer generated Icons, they were debriefing him on how and why he did what he did. The computer generated Icon that was of an alien species completely took John by surprised because it spoke to him in English. The species had no ears or mouth But he could still he speak and the humanoid can hear and understand John as he spoke back to it. "Hello my name is Kor-rey"; it said. Mr. Spectrum I am an advanced healer and I was recruited by this fe-loon because of my ability to heal others. John stuttered back; "hello". Mr. Spectrum While you were on that planet you was infected by a mite. John heard the word infection and did a double take, "excuse me"; he said. You were infected with a spore that is attacking your dust mites. John looked at him with wonderment on his face. "I have dust mites?" "Yes you do Kor-rey;" said.

John was yet amazed again. "I was only on the planet surface for only a few hours before being teleported up here". Before John could say anything further, Kor-rey said;" each and every time you are teleported you are scanned to make sure that you are not rematerialized with the clothes you are wearing and the equipment you have on fused to your cells. We scanned you and you have an anomaly growing on your skin. It is attacking the dust mites that are living on you. These spores are rapidly, attacking and destroying the mites on your skin and it will attack your skin then eventually kill you, the spores move on a molecular and microscopic level. John did not need no more convincing he said; "Kor-rey, is it"? The Alien made the universal head nod for yes. "Please; you need not say any more".

He and the computer icons walk toward another undescriptive room; it had another capsule that was standing up right that look like a casket too. This was black in color, and felt like it was made of a different metal. It stood in great contrast to the room that was stainless steel with a large area view port that allowed space to be seen from this room. John looked at Kor-Rey and said; "how long would I have to be in here"? Kor-rey said; "unfortunately for the duration of the trip to your home world". John thought about it he said; "On the transit cycle here I had training, I was occupied." "I won't be able to survive mentally in that capsule for that long". Kor-rey thought about. It was a computer Icon; it was computing the correct solution for John's conundrum. "We have a crown that stimulates your neurons, and implants thoughts and feelings directly into your brain." Kor-rey said. "This crown was used to manipulate and interrogate prisoners, when we use to actually do that sort of thing." "We cannot read your mind, so we can not implant thoughts into it." "You will have to entertain yourself with your own thoughts; while the crown fires your neurons, and read your brain waves it will stimulate your hypothalamus and the other senses in your brain." "You dream it you create it." John thought to himself may imagination is pretty "much out there"! John said; "Thank you Kor-rey," John walks over to the black casket, slowly because he was not completely sure. "Relax, relax, he kept saying to himself over and over again. If that fe-loon wanted you dead you would have been dead, a long time ago." John made, it to the black casket as he walk over to it. Kor-rey produces the crown out of thin air, but John new better it was teleported to his Alien hands. Kor-rey handed the crown to John. John looks at the crown. It was a small and delicate, band of gold. It was not ornate at all just like everything else around the capsule. The fe-loons have evolved away from ostentation in things that they create. The importance on functionality versus how it looks won out as their evolution took place. John placed the delicate, gold band on his head. Kor-rey motioned for him to enter the capsule; so John did. As the casket closed, John closed his eyes and tries to imagine something nice as he settles in for decontamination. He closed his eyes and was astonished to see himself in his favorite vacation spot. It was 80° degrees and the moon was full. The city was all a buzz. The black asphalt was wet because the city street cleaning trucks just made their final run for the night. John looks down over across the street from where he is standing he sees a building he has not seen before he has been here over a hundred times and don't remember this particular club. He looked down at himself and realized he was dressed in a tuxedo. The men and women going to this club were also formally dressed. So he followed the crowd and went into the club. The club was beautiful it had crush velvet couches and chairs, huge chandeliers, large flowing curtains. There was priceless works of art and erotic art. It was amazing. The outside of the building gave no clue of the grandeur of the inside of the building. As John watch the spectacle of well-dressed people parade around in a vanity fair. John saw a woman walk by him naked from the waist down. She was incredibly attractive and she was handing out tickets. She eventually walked over to John gave

John a ticket. John said, "Thanks; what's this for." She said; "this is for the female glory-hole room upstairs". Perhaps you would like the male room"? John said "no;" and vigorously shook his head. "Thank you", he said. She said "no problem". "The new shift is going to start in five minutes". I just got off of shift, maybe we can run into each other tomorrow I can tell by your physique you'll give me a good pounding." John, blushed, and said; "Maybe," and watched her walk away as he felt a full range of emotions; from embarrassment to arousal, he mingled all over the room. Every one was attractive. No matter how old he or she was. Every one was well dressed, and moved with the poise of an athlete. John thought to himself, this is a really nice place I got to come back here. The ticket that was given to him began to hum and vibrate, as the lights around its edges started to pulse on and off. John look around, there was only stairwell going up. There was a large group of men walking down the left side of the stair well. They looked wore out as if they were running a 5K marathon. John walked to the right and watches his step as he ascended the large grand stair case that had brass hand rails and red carpet all the way up to the landing on the second floor. As he went up stairs he could noticed there is a group of elevators; that the others took as they walked up the stairs pass the glory hole room. John paid the least of his attention to the elevators. He looks around the large room as he tried to burn every sight and sound into his permanent memory. Women were laying on small tables with their feet up in stir ups, the tables were made in such away where the woman's back was supported and the man enjoying her lower half can walk up and enter her without difficulty. It was incredible all the holes were occupied with females. To the left women were lying in missionary position. The right of the room the women were in doggie style waiting for some attention. All the way in the rear of the room, behind the stair case there were glory holes. The holes were large for a man to put in his whole hook-up into and there were rails and handles on the walls for a person to hold onto as he was being pleasured. John stood there and could not move because he was shocked by his own sub-conscious thoughts. It was his fantasy; he thought, 'I should as well enjoy it'. He walks over to the waitress and ask her for a beer, she said; "Yes sir," John could not pick; they were all well rounded, and perfect. They were all different shapes and colors, some of the men were licking the women's vaginas before they went in; others had their on lube with them. John walked over to the holes in the back of the room the waitress brought him his beer. He unfolded a 100 hundred dollar bill and placed it on her tray. He walked from scene to scene, enjoying the sights and sounds as he went. He decided he was going to get warmed up first. He went over to the holes in the back of the room he undid his pants and placed his Balls and hard dick in one of the unoccupied holes. He noticed the hole was made for action. He waited in anticipation and did not have to wait long. He felt a very warm and wet mouth on his cock. He gave a sudden involuntary reaction as he felt small hands grip the base if the shaft and held him in place as she went up and down; nice and steady not too fast, not too slow. She was like a machine. Up and down, in and out; he felt her tiny tongue licking the head of his penis. John dropped his beer as he was brought to a very happy ending after two minutes of skillful stimulation. John felt weak in the knees as he headed over and tried to try and pick up his beer that was fizzing out and spilling all over the floor. He was embarrassed and looks around; no one was watching him. Everyone else was having their own happy endings. He adjusted himself and zipped up his pants and walked over to the couch in the middle of the room. When he got there, he sat on the very comfortable couch and he nodded off and went to sleep.

As John fell asleep in his day dream he physically fell asleep; he was unconscious and his mind did wonder. He dreamt about being married with Kids, to being the President of the United States. The Alien Kor-rey interrupted John self-induced slumbering and informed him they are now in his home solar system, and that his decontamination will end a few hours and to prepare himself for his teleportation back to his penthouse, and his problems. Thought; "Well, it was fun while it lasted. What could I dream up now"?

John thought about it long and hard, and he settled on a fantasy that will never come true. John use to climb into the crawl spaces up in the girls cabin at summer camp. He went back to that fond memory. Her name was Emery Johnson she was 18 years-old, when John was 13; John never seen a grown woman naked before. She was athletic, his height, and beautiful. She had everything in all the right places she was a perfect specimen of a woman. John concentrates on this fantasy he starts off standing on the softball field staring at the girl's cabins. He knew where she was, cottage

C. He stood there and watches her as she walked out of her cabin and went into the shower cabin. John walked over to the shower cabin. It was a stroll because the softball field was on a hill, and John had to walk through a small wooded area that was left uncut & give the girls some privacy and to act as a barrier for us walking 'hard-ons'. John walked through the wooded area; he noticed it had a path. Apparently he was not the only boy who made this quest. He walked up to the female shower; he heard the shower, and the laughing and talking of the girls in the other cabins as they settle down for the right. John slowly walked by the other cabins. He could fell this humidity from the steam, and see the slight glow from the moonlight as the sky turned from day to night. His heart was racing and his thirteen year-old manhood was so hard he could cut rock with it. John walked in to the shower and saw her clothes and towels lying on a bench as he walked further into the shower cabin until he could see her washing herself through the steam. John was standing there when she saw him. She did not say a word she motion for him to come nearer and he came. It was just as he thought it would be; she grabbed him I pulled him toward her. She took over, all the sexual aggression John showed women during, his many trysts and encounters, she showed toward him. She kissed him with an opened full mouth. She held him in her arms as she worked the shaft of his penis; she said; "eat me", and forcefully push John down in between her legs. She buried his face in side of her pussy. John knew what time it was, and licked her on the pink inside of her vagina. He left her labia and clitoris alone. He licked her where he thought her pee-hole was. John licked her nice and long. She had her back against the wall she howled like a cat in heat as she wrapped her left leg over his right shoulder. She held him tight and let him please her until she was tired. She looked at him when he stood up and gave him a mischievous smirk as she turned around and let John hit it from the back. She bent over and let John own it. He was smacking is hips against her buttocks. It was a loud flesh to flesh noise that can be heard over the running showers. John kept his thrusting up for a while his legs were tired and he started to feel the fatigue in his lower back. He kept up his constant in and out motion. His body was starting to react, he continued as his legs started to wobble, and he pulled it out at the last second and blew cum all over the small of her back. She was smiling as she turned around. John was tired like, he just worked all day long. She smile and kiss him and pull his ear closed to her mouth and said, "John", don't tell anybody, get out of here before you get caught. She walk away John picked up his wet T. Shirt and Shorts and ran out through the front of the shower and through the wooded park that was created by many other hot blooded and horny teenage boys like him. John pulled that wet T-shirt over his head and tried to put his wet shorts on while he was running. When he got his first leg into his shorts, he was hopping on the second. His sneakers were wet and he fell face first down a slight depression heading for a cluster of poison oak. John snapped back into reality and awoke out his erotic dream right before he landed in poison oak. He felt his heart race. He was sweating and his body felt like he just had sex. This crown that he gave was incredible. John sat there and waited the 40 or so minutes for him to exit from the casket. He was only away for less than a week; but he travelled to another planet in another galaxy and fought for his life to help save a group of fellow humans from the Curse of slavery, and experimentation. "Wow," He thought I am going to relax and take a mini - vacation before football season. I also have to defend my heavy weight Championship Belt; I got a full plate. As he thought more about what he was going to do when he got home. The casket open without warning Kor-rey and the colonel's computer Icons were standing there waiting on him to exit. The large host of Icons that he was not formally introduced to that played some type of support role in his adventure was there; and as usual, they did not speak to him because it was not necessary. They were arranged in the same procession when he first was introduced to the space capsule. The Colonel said; thank you. John, we would like to discuss you helping us in the future. John said; "Colonel Thank you," but I have a career to get back to." I have a full plate as well, as you know; before John could finish his thought pattern, he was moving to take the gold crown off his head. He said; "Colonel how much for this crown. I remember being told that you don't use it anymore. Colonel said; "that crown is not for sale, that crown as very old and obsolete compared to newer created apparatuses on this capsule, with that being said." "You don't have enough money to buy that capsule". John said; "well can I use it"? The Colonel smirked; "you have I life to get back to." The Colonel said, "Your new United States government needs you and they want to use you to give them information on the fe-loon that recruited you for this mission.

John said, "Oh, I thought I was going to go home and he left it alone". The Colonel said; "I am afraid not." You are a powerful man. Now, you are a man who has a fe-loon's confidence." John you are human, the fe-loons know your name. He would probably negotiate with you and work out a deal for you for that device you hold." Kor-rey walked up to John put his hand out and John reluctantly gave him back the crown. John was surprised at how hard that was. He said Colonel; "I don't know if I could make any commitments, but I truly did like the adventure and the excitement. The Colonel said, "Well, if you need me you can teleport your voices sound up to the capsule and I could hear you. Please, be ready for anything because if we call you we are going to need you. This particular race of extra-terrestrial never speaks to other species; it is very possible that the fe-loon would never call you again in you life time. John relaxed a little. "Colonel, thank you for all you help and encouragement. John walks over the teleport apparatus and centered himself on it and was immediately back in his penthouse standing in front of him was the general and his secretary captain. There were two other people standing there also. This two wore suits and had on dark shades despite being inside of a building. Two white males, both were clean shaven one had a receding hair line and he looked to be the younger of the two. "Welcome back;" the General, said, followed immediately by the captain saying the same. The two suits were standing there staring at him as he stepped off of the apparatus. After John stepped off the apparatus the apparatus was immediately teleported away. The teleportation harness that he was wearing also dematerialized. John had the strangest sensation that he was standing there naked. John said; "how are you General, Captain, I don't mean to be rude, but I don't like people inviting themselves to my house". The older agent answered, this is an issue of national security; sir your civil liberties and your sense and sensibilities are dead last in importance. John responded and said; "are you fucking kidding me!" Get the hell out of my house!" The agent took off is shades and walks over to John in a very determined stride, the General stepped forward and said; "Gentleman"! Both the agent and John did not break eye contact. The General said; "this is agent Jones, and the man standing in front of you is Agent Lynchburg. John said; "General I would have come to you, if this is was not necessary". Lynchburg said; "this is a matter of national security"! "May be you don't hear so good!" John said; "get out of my house or I am going to throw you out." Agent Lynchburg said; "I like to see that happen"! The General said; "enough!" "We don't have time for this". We need you to brief us on what transpired and what you have learned." General you want a full accounting of what I have done, and where I have been you need to leave my house and allow me to recollect my thoughts. Lynchburg"! The General said. "That's fair enough". "Thanks John for your cooperation." I will see you first thing in the morning. Where would you like to meet Lynchburg said; "we will be back at 6:00 am and we will escort you to the desired and secure meeting place. You don't have a chose in the matter you will be placed in custody of you don't show up"! The General said; "John, I apologize". Agent Lynchburg walked and away and very rudely told the other agent less go and walked out of John's penthouse suite without closing the door." "General you don't have to apologize. I know the type. He is trying to establish himself, and is jockeying for position. He is over compensating for something. I deal with his type all day long as a pro athlete". The General nodded and said; "how was your trip?" John walks over and closed the door of his penthouse suite and asked the General and Captain to sit down. John began with small talk and told the General about his incredible journey. He went through in detail the incredible journey, the computer Icons on the capsule (Spaceship). He also described his training and how he learns how to use the teleporting apparatus in a matter of a few hours. General Timothy McCormick and his aid Captain Tiffany Morgan listen intently. John told him everything but; his pond bathing episode, and the crown he used to entertain himself. The General pulled out a small cigar, and absent mindedly lit; it and then realized his manners and said; "Sorry," you don't mind if I smoke do you? John said; "go ahead". Captain Morgan said; Mr. Spectrum our country needs you and needs you to give us any and all information that you have now and in the future about the alien's technology and information about the other planets you are going to visit in the future. John said; "I will try my best. That dummy who call himself Lynchburg would not get a "good morning" or a "how you are doing" out of me. He is the deputy commander of the C.I.A. branch office here in the mid west. Why, does the C.I.A. need a branch office in the Midwest? Captain Morgan smiled the C.I.A. has, as well as you know people every where. The Midwest post is the least busy and often times is staffed by people that the agency wants to get rid off. No pun intended. Lynchburg is a political appointee he is given a deputy position because of his politically connected family. He was sent out here so he can not cause any trouble. You just happened to be the most important thing that he has dealt with in his short career. Johnathan said; "Let me guess, I going to be dealing with him more often." The General and Captain answer simultaneously "yes"! I going to tell you right now I am not going to get up to 6 a.m. and I don't want him in my house. Tell him to back off. The General said; "fair enough;" 10 A.M. will do? John said; "yes." The General and Captain Morgan let John go so he can relax; John let them out and John checked his voice mails and E. Mails.

John woke up to the cell phone ringing, the next morning 7 A.M. He reaches over and picked up the phone. "Hello." "Hey baby, how you doing"? John knew who it was and he hung up. Damn, she is flipp'in crazy. I had sex with her one time she thinks she owes Mr. John could not go back to sleep so he got up. He got ready and put on one of his best suits and went to breakfast. John received a text from Capt. Morgan, the General's Mobile Command center has moved. He finished his breakfast signed a few autographs and left his favorite restaurant. It did not occur to John that he was being followed he was a famous athlete he should have known better. John pulled up into a parking lot of the local mall and went to the door of the command center. The command center was disguised as a contractor trailer. The workers repairing the parking lot was a good distraction; all of the road construction going on in the Detroit Metropolitan area was common and people won't think twice about it. John walks into the trailer the outside gave no clue of how posh and how high-tech the inside was. Lynchburg was waiting on him he had an angry pouting look on his face. John looked at him, and thought to himself; "this guy ain't got no man traits." The General and Captain were there, Lynchberg was there. He watching John's every movement and was looking for any reason at all to say something. "Thanks for coming", the General said and motioned for John to sit down. John sat down. Lynchberg made it a point to sit down next to John as close as possible. John felt uncomfortable as John was eyeing Lynchberg and his unusual body language. The wall of the trailer started to blink. Then it shown the word stand-by; a few second later the satellite-uplink booted up and John could see the secretary of defense, and the national security advisor and the director of the C.I.A. in a room that had the American flag and the seal of the United States of America on a partition behind them. Before the director started to speak Lynchburg cut him off. How are you gentlemen doing? The director's face blazed with anger at Lynchburg and shut him down with out a word. Lynchburg cowed down to his better as all eyes and ears focused on Johnathan Spectrum.

"Mr. Spectrum, thank you for coming" the director said. The director made it a point to introduce the secretary of defense and the National Security Advisor to the president. He was formal and professional, and he did not mention Lynchburg who was sitting there biting his lower lip as a child being picked last for basketball. They ignored him if he was a child. John thought to himself, this is going to be long boring and irritating.

Mr. Spectrum we asked you to come here today becaus.e of your unique ability and quite frankly; because you are one of the few human beings that has actual contact with extra-terrestrial life. We need you to tell us everything no matter how small a detail it may be. The need for secrecy is paramount. We have a lot of questions especially about the Alien. John interrupted "the Fe-loon", he said. "That's what it calls himself?" John said; "Yes, Mr. Spectrum what does it look like?" John said; "I did not meet with the E.T. face to face it communicated with me through a array of computer Icons, control by it, that I believe were of real living beings at one time. The three men looked absolutely riveted on every word. "Bull Shit!" Agent Lynchburg said. John looks at him and did not say a word. He turned back to the three men on the satellite up link. "I thought I was being questioned and not interrogated." "I could leave and come back with a lawyer." Agent Lynchburg was

flushed with a combination of anger and embarrassment"
Agent Lynchburg said; "Excuse me! You are going to tell
the truth or do we have to be interrogated by you. "Agent
Lynchburg"!! The director of the C.I.A. screamed! Shut
up! John said; "I can't do this all day; either he leaves or I
leave"! John said; just as loud, just as angry. "Mr. Spectrum
we apologize for the rudeness of our subordinate. Please,
stay. Agent Lynchburg we no longer require your presence
you can leave". Agent Lynchburg looks at Johnathan with
an anger laced with jealousy. He turned backed to The
General and the Captain and said in a whiny voice; "how
come they get to stay?"

The three high ranked government officials were annoyed more than
anything. The director of the C.I.A. was more embarrassed now at this
unprofessional and obvious childless behavior displayed by one of his
senior officers. He looked backed and did not say a word. Agent Lynchburg
got up in a loud and undignified manner; staring back at the three annoyed
professionals. He looks at John and walks out of the construction trailer
like a potty child. "Mr. Spectrum we again apologize but, money and
politics make strange bed fellows." John continued, "I stopped at the
computer Icons." "Yes," was said in unison by all three of the men waiting
for him to continue his report. John said; "I did not meet directly with the
Fe-loon it communicated with me indirectly, "I was communicating with

an Icon. The Icons were of different alien species. They were astonished at his proclamation, he continued. There were three computers Icon that spoke to me. One was of an alien species; I was not rude and didn't ask him what he called his people. But, he was bi-pedal, and he had two eyes and ears. His skin was turquoise he had a snout instead of a nose. "He," John stopped excuse me gentlemen", I am assuming that it was a "he". It was 7½ ft. tall and thin and it head was two times larger than my own. There were two others, a colonel from the Confederate States of America. "What"?! The Secretary of Defense said. John look at him directly; there was a computer Icon that was a Confederate Colonel. He was my primary contact. The three men were shocked beyond reason. He was a man slightly shorter than me he was in his later thirties he looked a lot older he was a wealthy slave owner from Louisiana. The men were hanging on every word now. His name was Colonel Sawyer; they did not give away signs of surprise when John mentioned his name. John described the small framed doctor that helped him with his initial orientation and prepared him for the Fe-loons tasks. John went to describe the capsule the pods, the drones that went into the pyramid with him. The pyramid itself, and the bio-engineered half-eagle half-men and women hybrids; the unspeakable horrors of the waste disposal area. The Japanese solider from Imperial Japan; he described his physical attributes and his fighting ability and how lucky he was to be standing in front of them now. John was talking so much He lost all track of time his butt was starting to get swore from sitting for so long. He stretch in his chair and rubbed the back of his neck.

"I hope that the information that I gave you can help you. I am eager to get on with my life. Please don't consider me rude or selfish; I got a $250 million dollar a year career to think of. As an athlete I probably got seven to ten years shelf life before I start to expire so-to-speak. The men slightly smiled at his small joke.

"Mr. Spectrum you are a treasure trove of Intel about other parts of the known an unknown universe and about E.T. life beyond our understanding"; said the National Security Advisor. "Your unique ability that we were not known to us, until now makes you into a very valuable asset." John looked puzzled; "what my athletic ability"? He said; "No, your mental defenses, that God gave you. There is no way to test a human being for such a unique gift. We have an older woman in our employ that has happen to be the strongest and most consistent telepath in our history of dealing with psionic powered human beings. You have an ability that makes you impervious to all telepathic intensions including suggestion and or domination." John was curious and asked; "What's domination". We attempted to test your abilities, you have no idea that you have been under psionic attacked several times at the first meeting." John started to think back that old lady in the leather jacket with piercings". He was thinking it and, said it out loud. "Yes sir," he heard from one of men in the satellite uplink but did not know who said it. He was so embroiled in his on inner thoughts. Even though John was immune to psionic attack, he was angry for the attacking any way. Johns facial expressions changed and his tone. The men in the other satellite uplinked area heard and pick up on the slight inflection of his tone and body language. John said; "Gentlemen, I am done, I am glad I can help you". "Mr. Spectrum, we would like to contract with you for unique skills and consult you whenever you are contacted again". Johnathan turned to the General and Captain and turned backed to the three men of rank and power. "We can discuss that possibly, I can no longer stay; you gentlemen and lady have a good day". John got up and walked out of the secured area that was shielded from electronic intrusion, tried the door it was immediately unlocked when he turned at the only two occupants in the trailer with him. John was annoyed at being attacked psionically his mood was compounded by being hungry; he spent the whole morning being debriefed. He was immediately bombarded with questions and accusations by Lynchburg who was waiting for him to come out. He stepped in front of John pointing his finger. In a loud whiny tone, "You are going to respect me and my position!" John looked at him more annoyed and did not slow his pace or move to one side. He bumped Lynchburg hard as he passed him. Lynchburg said; "I will destroy you; you ain't anybody important." John stopped and turned around and walked backed toward Lynchburg. He knew how to handle his type; he dealt with this type of personality all day long in the locker rooms and the football fields. As he walked back toward Lynchburg he watch Lynchburg straighten his ruffled suit and straighten his tie. He was not a very confident man John could tell; because he refused to make I contact as he walked toward him.

John walked up to him, stood in front of him and Lynchburg turned his face up toward him in a vain attempt to look brave. John said; "The C.I.A. director wanted to see you immediately after I left; why are you still standing here"? The Dummy Lynchburg eyes widened in fear as he ran back toward the trailer and bumped his face into the trailer door as he tried to run into it and it was locked. John turned around and walked away as Lynchburg pounded on the door and trying to pull the door open. John got into his car and drove away from the construction site. There is a lot of truth in what my grandfather told me as his turned on to Ford Rd to go home. "A man that does not work for or earn what he gets, he does not know his true potential".

Mr. Lynchburg was such a man, where everything was given to him as a child; so he is the type of man that thinks everyone is just suppose to give him things.

John prepared for his next title defense. John has been the Heavy Weight Champion for 2 years now. He planned to keep it that way. John got several calls from Capt. Morgan and he is beginning to enjoy her company and small talk.

John was now with is trainers in an old Recreational Center in Detroit. He bought it when it was condemned; he put over $ 3 million dollars into it to rehabilitate it. He also bought over $ 125,000 of new equipment and opened it to public. His trainers were Darren Johnson; Derick Jones (D.J) and Frank Williams. These guys have been with John from the beginning as much as they get on his nerves, he would never replace them because they were indispensable. D.J. was holding the heavy bag while John was throwing his best punch combinations into it. He heard a large commotion and John turned around. It was a local news crew that he knows personally. The lead reporter Jacqueline Smith is a real vendetta against John. He does not give interviews; and it is if she took it personal.

Mr. Spectrum! Mr. Spectrum! Are you prepared to answer the allegations of what you have done! John stop hitting the heavy bag; and turned to her and said; "What allegations." The security guard was an old man in his seventies and he could not stop or hold back the determined woman. Jacqueline Smith turned to the news camera, which was on as she was giving a live report. "What allegations." John snapped; "I swear, if ain't one thing it is another", as he thought to himself, he took a towel and wiped the sweat off his face. "You are accused to raping a woman"; she said. Just then he heard his cellphone ring. John said; "what, I have being training hard for the last 2 weeks I haven't raped nobody". She was amused by his anger and knew she had an exclusive interview. She has been following him for the past couple of weeks and she conveniently knew where he was going to be when a press conference was called by the district attorney saying that Mr. Spectrum was wanted in questioning in a rape of a Beatty Tomlin; John did not know anything about this and was completely blind sided. "You are aware that there is a warrant out for arrest!" she said. She had a very large smile on her face as she watched his facial expressions change from anger and arrogance to fear and surprise. John said; "What!" again. He knew better and refused to speak any further. "I have no comment;" he said; "You have to talk to my lawyer." She persisted, "Your fans have a right to know what happened, the public has a right to know what happened." John said; "No comment more forcefully; as he saw more reporters and camera men rush into the gym. "She would not relent. John stepped out of the ring and began to put on his sweat hoodie and grabbed his gym bags. John picked up his ringing cell phone. His agent was on the other end angry and flustered! "John we got a problem!" "What's going on"? "One of your many groupies has accused you of rape, you need to leave the gym, they are going to publicly embarrass you and arrest you on live television". Jacqueline Smith acting and behaving as if she won the lottery and stepped in front of John, with a microphone in his face, and he then side-stepped her with the physical agility of a pro-bowler; He walked away from the crowds of people as they shouted questions at him and called his name. Darren, D.J. and Frank was trying to hold the crowd back as John walked out of the gym he purposely left the building via back door and left his jag - in the parking lot. He hopped the bus and went to the downtown Police Precinct. He got to the police precinct and walked up to the front desk and identified himself and turned himself in. John was angry, embarrassed and afraid at the same time he never been arrested before. The desk sgt. walked up to him and said; "this way". The desk sgt. led him to a back interrogation room, where he waited. While he was on the bus he told his agent what his intentions were. He told her to meet him at the police station. He was sitting in the interrogation room feeling queasy. When the two detectives walked in they were looking very much like the stereotype; of coffee drinking donut eating cops. One was smiling and the other had a scowl that looked permanent. "Hi, I am Detective Hopkins, and this is my partner Detective C. Brown." Hopkins said. Mr. Spectrum thank you for coming in, so how are you doing"? Hopkins was talking when his partner in a raised and agitated voice said. "You going down, we got a slam dunk case against you"! John was like; "What case; what am I being accused of, and who is the accuser"? Beatty Tomlin he yelled; it's in your best interest to come clean now!" John looked at him incredulously and did not say a word. Hopkins chimed in, in a cordial and respectful tone. It is true Mr. Spectrum you are in a bind, we have a credible witness, and your D.N.A." Hopkins and Brown were waiting for a reply and John sat there waiting on his lawyer and reviewing his options mentally. "Well," C. Brown said. John shrugged his shoulders at him and kept his mouth closed. They both became a little more annoyed the 'good cop', bad cop cliché was not working like they expected. Contract negotiations, weight-ins, press conferences gave John the experience he needed to sit there and not say a word while his adversary, whether it was another fighter or lawyer for the other side grill him and try and manipulate him into hasty decisions. John let Hopkins and C. Brown goat him, coerce, suggest and hint all they wanted and John did not say a word. Detective Hopkins said; "Can I get you some coffee"? John said; "No, thanks." So Mr. Spectrum how long have you been fighting for." Hopkins conversation was very good, he switch virtual gears from the allege accusations to small talk and back to the accusations. John saw the slight direction change in the conversation and he clamed up again. John was not just any dumb jock. The two detectives were beginning to imply threats when a knock on the door got all of their attention; John's agent walked in with three lawyers that he never seen before. John's agent gave him a reassuring nod, and said; "Gentlemen, please direct all your questions to Mr. Spectrum's legal team. The two detectives were a lot smoother in their delivery with Johns lawyering team than they were with him. His lawyers, all Caucasian, one woman, very attractive with her hair in a bun, she had that super sexy Librarian look. The other two were obvious father and son. The booth had red hair and freckles the father was a whole 12 inches shorter than his son. They both wore classes and had the same type of blue business suit. The police officers were not fazed by the professional looking lawyer team. John's agent was wearing her hair up with a very short mini skirt. That was color contrast with her suit jacket; she wore heels and looked quite alluring. The detectives were basically trying to portray themselves as professional. They were experienced at this type of questioning, they were use to dealing with ordinary people who they could intimidate and coerce with trickery. Johns legal team was all poker faced, when the lieutenant and Asst. District Attorney walked in. The two detectives stopped talking. The Assistant D.A. was as cocky as they came. He had a stupid grin on his face as if; he was looking at easy prey. The D.A. was a short black American man with a cleft palette; he was wide at the shoulders and looks real goofy in his loud green suit with black pen stripes and colorful tie. He was just as dumb as he looked. "Johnny"! How you doing, we finally meet at last." John did not say a word he remained stoic, and did not betray his emotions. The D.A. let his anger show; because he thought he was a lot more important than he was. He said in a high pitch voice; "Hi"! John looked at him and said;" talk to my attorneys don't speak to me". The D.A. said; "I am John Baptist and you gonna respect me". He sniffed loud, rubbed his thumb across his wide nose, and grabbed his crotch! The two detectives were looking around if they were embarrassed and they were. The lieutenant was standing there with both his eyebrows raised looking at this freak show called Assistant County Prosecutor John Baptist representing the Wayne County Prosecuting Office. John watches in actual annoyance as this obviously unqualified person, who got his position because of his family or political connections give him a speech on reality. You can tell that the two detectives who tried to interrogate John alone were more annoyed than he was. John's attorney Mr. Carlston the father and lead attorney of attorney team Carlston and Son spoke up; he looked like a frail old man, but his strength was in his litigation skills, interrupted by raising his index finger. What is my client being charged with"; he said while he took off his reading glasses and began to clean them. There was no immediate answer from the peanut galley! He said again; "What is my client being charged with?" The assistant D.A. Baptist said; "we have a young woman whom alleges Mr. Spectrum raped her in his downtown loft". Johnathan's attorney was poker faced as he put his glasses back on, "What is he being charged with?" The Lieutenant said; "Mr. Spectrum is not under arrest he was wanted for questioning he has not been charged with any crime as of yet." We have a victim, whom is alleging that you raped her yesterday; we would like you to tell us where you were yesterday at 9:00 pm. The lieutenant looked at Johnathan Spectrum expecting him to answer, Johnathan's attorney answered for him with a question; what physical evidence do you to support these allegations. Assistant D.A. John Baptist said; "We don't need any"! "I am going to lock yo' punk ass up!" Every person in the room turned and looked at the D.A. The two detectives were so angry they were both either biting their lips or holding their breathe trying not to blurt out any foul words at the D.A. The lieutenant looks at Baptist and lowers his head in to his hands. John's attorney said, "We thank you sir for your candor." Mr. Spectrum will be leaving." "Mr. Spectrum you can go; as he turned toward John. D.A. Baptist run to the door and blocked his exit; "you only leave when we say you can leave." Mr. Carlston Jr. exploded; "you are in violation of my clients rights. You cannot hold him against his will without probable cause and or evidence!" Get the hell away from that door, or we will file a criminal complaint against you for kidnapping and sue the Wayne County Prosecuting Offices for vicarious liability!" The D.A. was lost for words. The lieutenant walks over and opens the door with the D.A. standing in front of it. The Assistant D.A. relented as the door was opened he forcefully pushed by the Assist. D.A.; "Mr. Spectrum we apologized for the inconvenience." No one in the room said anything as John walked out with his agent. John walked out of the police station as all of the police officers and the criminals stared at him. He walks right into a gaggle of news reporters and camera crews. John and his agent ignored their questions, and heckling from the bystanders. He got into the limo - and his agent raised the privacy screen. "We got to address the public." "Why"? John said. "Your fans need to know what is going on." "I am going to schedule a press conference so you can address these allegations." "No you are not" John said. "Well you need to answer these questions; you are being broadcasted right now on live news". She turned on the T.V. in the limo as John watch he watch the limo moving through the downtown Detroit streets as it was being followed by a helicopter. As the limo enter the Freeway. He turned off the T.V. and said; "Where are we going?" "We are going to Carlston office." John said; "No, I'm not; take me home!" "We need to talk about what's going on; you need to stop acting arrogant, and give a few interviews. John shot back I am not arrogant!" I resent being called a sell out because I am independently wealthy or being private!" "You work for me! It is not the other way around! I pay you $2.5 million dollars a year; I can get another agent just like you can get another client; now take me home!" "John," she said; in a mild tone, I am here for you". John snapped back; "You don't hear so good, "Take me home." John sat back and did not say another word as his agent directed the driver to take John back to his loft. John was fuming, all the way back. He got out of the limo and did not wait for the driver to open his door. He was immediately bombarded with reporters, cameras, he ignored them all. He walks into his front gate and immediately walked to his front door. His loft was an old factory it was beautiful. The old parking lot was surrounded by a wall, Johns; architect had the sense to plant hanging veins on the wall to keep the graffiti artist away. The outside of his loft was remarkably unchanged from the original factory's design.

He spent over $10 million dollars on the grounds and landscaping and has spent nearly $50 million dollars making it into a luxury oasis in the middle of old Detroit. John was critisized of course for being a sell out, and "Not keeping it real." At first he was critisized for not giving any thing back to his community, then he was critisized for not using local contractors when he got his loft built. Then he was critisized for rubbing his wealth in the noses of the people he was trying to relate to and support with his tax money by not leaving his community. John thought to himself "I can't take this; who would accuse me of raping them when I have went to great pains to mess around with women I only know"? John turned on the T.V. to watch the news. He watched the so call legal experts talk about something none of them knew about. "This is news?" he thought. "Colonel" John said it and thought his name, and pictured his computer icon in his mind at the same time. "The Colonel said; "Yes." John was surprised at how clear his voice was. "Colonel," are you eaves dropping on me"? The Colonel said; "no; I hear you when you want to be heard. John said; "Oh." Colonel I am having some problems." I need to relax, could I borrow that golden crown that the Kor-rey let me used while I was decontaminating. Mr. Spectrum the crown is physically addictive if it is used for pleasure; and you will not want to come out of your subconscious and face reality. This is the reason why it was not used anymore by the race that created; with any tool there are Dangers to be avoided. "Colonel, I have a good life in the present, I am having some bad luck right now and I need a distraction. "What are your problems"? The colonel said. "I am being accused to sexual assault by someone and I don't know where this accusation is coming from or what to do about it". The Colonel said; "hmmm! You need more than a crown you need help. The Colonel said; "we have an Icon who specializes in covert espionage; spying that sort of thing we can help you". John was so moved he could not speak. "Colonel I don't know how to thank you." "No thanks is needed we need you in the near future. It appears that the members of you government has been trying to make contact with the fe-loon ever since you undertook your mission they have been trying to use you and they want the fe-loons attention. This sexual assault episode might be an attempt to force you personally; you in your time call it 'leverage'. In my time we call it 'black mail'; have you seen the accuser yet"? John answer, "No." The colonel said; "exactly". The Colonel said; "the Icon that is programmed for espionage her name is Natasha." I will get her on the case and I will contact you with any new information". The moment when the colonel stop talking was when the crown was teleported to him, it materialized at eye level, and at arm's reach. John reaches out and took the crown out of mid-air. John looked at the crown he felt guilty for wanting to visit the dark desires of his sub-conscious, but he had to get away from his problems at least for the time being. John could not think of any thing that was extra-ordinary in the sex department. He had no ideas or fetishes that he could experiment with so he put the crown on his head and will himself to surprise himself.

He opens his sub-conscious to college. He was walking through campus and was watching the other students do the same. He look down and realized he was wearing pajamas and slippers, and he look around slightly concerned about how weird he may look walking around campus and 7:45 at night in pajamas and slippers. He was relieved to see several of his male and female co-eds wearing their sleeping clothes walking to the same frat house. He looked at the house at he got closer it was his old frat house, we were having our annual 'Pajammy Jam.' John was laughing to himself as he walks in, he did not have to pay cover; he did not have to stand in line like every one else. He walks in and saw his old buddies, old friends and enemies for that matter and his buddy Paul who was killed in a car accident. He was taken aback by it all. The loud talking the stupid frat hand shake he have not seen or done in years. This was a good memory or half a memory anyway. John drank and smoked weed, and was feeling really good toward midnight. The girls started to get loose too. John walks up to this cute blonde that Paul was making out with on the dance floor. He put his hand right under her skirt and started rubbing her coochie. She looked at John with a look of sexual devious and gave him a smirk, pulled him closed and stuck her tongue down his throat. John and Paul were now both grinding on each one of her legs. She went from tongue kissing John to Paul and back again. The three of them were in the middle of the dance floor humping and grinding while every one else was humping and grinding. The dance floor was packed, people were bumping in to each other, as they danced and had a good time. No one was paying attention to John and Paul as they pulled up her pajama skirt and pulled down her bottoms. They then pulled her little girls panties down to her thighs. The two of them took turns finger banging her. John was so bold to put his middle finger in her booty hole. She turned slowly on John after she was kissing Paul. Paul held her while she was kissing John. Paul was fingering her in the front while John was fingering her in the back. All of a sudden she stops pulled her panties up and pulled her skirt down. John thought he went too far and the fun was over. Quite the contrary, after she adjusted her clothes see grabbed both of them by their dicks and led them up stairs. The whole party degenerated in to a drunken E-pilled fueled sex fest. Every room that they went into was occupied; they went into one room with four couples going at it like it was the end of the world. They went all the way up to the third floor, the attic. The attic was converted into a theater room. This is where they held their frat meeting and watch pornos; as the trio went into the theater room, they came upon a group of guys, five to be exact waiting on their turn for a blowjob. This super sexy girl was another cutie-pie. She was on her hands and knees naked from the waist down. She was sucking every dude in the room. They were all lying on the floor against the wall waiting their turn with their erections in their hands. She was enjoying herself. They saw how wet her pussy was. She was taking care of the third guy when they walked in. Her ass was up in the air her labia was swollen from her high state of arousal. The light from the hall way showed the three new comers that the room they chose was being used. The girl they were with did not care. She pulled them both into the room, and slammed the door before anyone could complain. The girl that was the center of attention did not skip a beat she kept going and the guys went back to their anxious anticipations. John, Paul and the unnamed blonde that Paul found went right to it. It was a repeat of what happened on the dance floor. This time she took her panties completely off, and tied them around her wrist. She squatted down and swallowed John's man hood. When she swallowed she swallowed. The insides of the throat was warm and as she slowly pulled his dick out of her throat he could feel her gag reflex opening and closing on the tip of his penis. She did Paul the same way. "This is one hell of a party, John thought." She pleases both of them her oral skills were incredible she stood up, and John turned her toward the wall and she assumed the position of a person getting arrested. She took all of his pounding and sexual aggressions. He put his right hand over her shoulder blade, and his left hand under her left hip. He was in a state of euphoria, the girl on the other side of the room with her pussy in the air, the five dudes watching him, the smell of marijuana smoke the sounds of the party going on down stairs. John's happy ending came in another titanic explosion. He pulled out at the very last moment and shot his wad all over her back as he grunted and groan like a cave man. John was covered in sweat as John collapse against the wall and watch Paul go at it. Paul turned her around to face him he held her up, both legs right and left were loosely wrap around his waist; as he held her up he used the wall supported her body weight. Paul made John feel inadequate Paul gave that girl a nice 35 minute long thrashing. Paul stopped and he started jerking off he stuck his dick in her mouth as he slowly came. She spat his cum on the floor, and with a smile she stood up. We all embraced each other one at a time, "John said; "thanks, for coming to our party". She said; "thanks for inviting me". She untied her panties from her wrist, put them back on and left. John looked at Paul and said, "Where you meet her at"? Paul said; "here, I thought she was one of your girls." "No John said; "I never seen her before." "Wow, we have one hell of story to tell don't we." Paul said; "Yeah, we do". Paul and John left the room. The girl that was giving head was stilling sucking another dude when they left. John went out into the back yard of the frat house and took a piss on the fence like all the other dudes were. The rest of the evening John laughed and joked with Paul. John knew that after Paul graduated he would never see him again. The party was now over and John knew he had to leave; with deep resignation he left the frat house and his sub-conscious never to see his college buddy Paul again.

John was actually physically tired from partying and hanging out with his old frat buddies. He hadn't realized how much he missed Paul until his sub-conscious brought him back up. John did not will the crown away he put it in his wall safe for safe keeping "Colonel;" John said, "Please don't be angry I am going to hold on to the crown for a while." The Colonel said; "I'm a computer Icon, why would I be angry over obsolete technology"? John thought about how much sense that made. He was walking around his loft and was so bored he could not take it. He refused to watch TV or answer the phone because of the accusations of sexual assault alleged against him. John started playing with the teleportation apparatus. He left the bracelet on the table and will it to himself and to his surprise it teleported to him. He left it on the night stand and walk into the kitchen and teleported himself to the apparatus. He was surprised that he no longer needed to physically have the device on his person to teleport. Colonel, John said; "I never asked you what the limits on my teleportation were". "The only limits are the one that you put on yourself. You can teleport any object to you if you can physically see it, or now exactly where it is. If it is hidden you cannot teleport it to you. You can also teleport yourself to a place that you know if you have been there of course; and also in your line of sight. Not to mention the arsenal at your disposal." "Did you tell the United States government that you can teleport any weapon conceived by human minds to your fingertips?" "No, sir," John said; "they can't read my mind I think that information would make me the most dangerous human on the planet." "Actually no you would not be considered the most dangerous human on the planet." John thought about that revelation "who would be the most dangerous person on the planet"? The Colonel did not immediately answer. He said; "Do you remember that old woman that was wearing a leather jacket, and had piercings." John thought about it; "Yeah, I remember her"! "How do you know of her"? We used her before; she has an innate ability like you that no other human being was born with." I was born with the ability not to have my mind read or be dominated by hypnotic suggestion." I was born with that trait and did know I had it." "So was she, there is no human being on the planet that can resist her strong psionic powers but you." "Wow," John thought! Your government is controlling her by making her physically addicted to a synthetic drug that was created in a laboratory. She is controlled; but you are not. That is why I strongly believe that your recent legal struggles are manufactured this is an attempt to control and manipulate you to be used and ultimately to use you to spy on the fe-loon and to gather information on his advanced technology. John said; "I can be paid, I am after all a business man." "Paying for something is not the same as owning that something;" the Colonel said. John thought about it, and said; "I take great pains to be private, and go out of my way to fly under the radar." The Colonel hesitated. "Sorry, for that I had to access your period and cross reference 'flying under the radar' with privacy. I know what you mean now." You have to put yourself in the shoes of your United States government. The need for your skills and abilities are too great to allow you to wonder around unchecked. How can I avoid this train wreck before it happens?" "Cooperate;" the Colonel said. "When they contact you, be open as much as you can, and help whenever it is needed this will take away some of the fear in your governments clandestine services." John thought about it, and said; "Thank you, Colonel I would like to confide in you more often." The Colonel said; "Any time, there was a time when I would not conceive a black man being so intelligent and smart. Your people have come a long way. The nation has grown exponentially I would be honored to be your confidant. It is not every day that a man born in the 1800's can interact with a man born in the late 1980's. John said; "Colonel one day I would like to hear your story. I would like to know about the southern state you were born in and about your adventures during the civil war." The colonel paused; I am a computer Icon my memories, feelings, wants needs every thing has been recorded. I can remember every thing. Even the things I forgot I forgot. It would be hard for me to relive those dark days". John said; "I'm sorry Colonel; I had know idea; please forgive me." The Colonel said; there is nothing to forgive, I am eager to learn about you and your career as well. Mr. Spectrum you have a good night. I will contact you when Natasha has found enough information to find the source of your accuser." The Colonel's voiced ceased, and John felt that his presence was no longer with him. John cut on the 24 hour cable news and watches the news coverage of the so-called experts comment on his so-called case. John fell asleep when he could not bear to keep his eyes open.

John wake up the next morning at 600 am partly because he had a fitful sleep and second his girlfriend Wanda, was calling him. She was not screaming this time she was trying to have an intelligent conversation. "Hey, good morning;" she said. He said; "Hey, what's up"? Wanda said;" I heard about what happened do you want to talk about it". John thought about it;" I can't because of legal reasons". Wanda said; "Oh come on, you can trust me." Then she just came out with it, "did you do it"! John thought to himself, I should have known. She is trying to get into the middle of this mess he is knee deep in. She is either recording this conversation or someone is listening on the other end. It is a very strong possibility both may be true. "Wanda;" John said. We need to talk." She said; "I agree were do you want to meet." I can't take the pressure and the any further stress." Wanda was silent. John said; "I cannot be with you any more," Wanda screamed "What! I love you!" "Wanda, Wanda, John repeated over and over again. Calm down! Wanda shrieked, and managed an incoherent, "Why?" I can't be with you; I want a wife not a baby mama." It just ain't working for us. She went from victim to villain in a heartbeat. I know you did it, you are a man whom thinks women are your personal play things, and you are a pig!" John did not say anything further he just push end call on his phone, and did not answer any numbers he did not recognize on his caller I.D. John willed himself to the gym and was instantly teleported there. He finished his work out from yesterday; he still had to defend his heavy weight title after all.

John teleported back to his apartment; he was beginning to appreciate his new found ability. When he walked from his living room area to look at his security monitors in the other room; he noticed dirt on his white carpet. "Mr. Spectrum"; is what he heard. He turned around quickly more startled than and angry; but when he recognized it was Lynchburg and Agent Jones he was fighting mad. Lynchburg began; "Please to meet your acquaintance again Mr. Spectrum." John was pissed off to say the least but; he was suddenly reminded what the Colonel said about being a threat and to cooperate with the government agents." John looked from Lynchburg to Jones, and could not help to stare at the old woman in a leather jacket with piercings and tattoos, standing next to her was a man John never seen before. He looked like "shaggy"; but with a grimace for a facial expressions.

"How may I help you lady and gentlemen"? John said. Lynchburg piped up, as expected; "I needed to talk to you Mr. Spectrum." I would like to recruit you into I small band of heroes." Lynchburg was walking around John's penthouse loft like he lived there. That annoyed the hell out of John. John let the pestering go on. John had every intention on helping them out and being one of the so called heroes if it got him his life back; but he could not seem too eager. He knew the game that they are playing so he could not expose his hand. John looked at the woman with piercings; "I am going to see if my mind can't be read." John gave his best poker face. He waited for a while before he answered and said; "No"! Lynchburg smiled widens; right then and there John knew that the Colonel was right. This legal problem he was having was a ploy to leverage John's cooperation.

"Mr. Spectrum in light of your legal problems I don't think you can afford to turn me down." Lynchburg made such a strong emphasizes on the word 'me', John could not help but to notice. "Well;" John said, "I got a good legal team and it got a good alibi." Lynchburg was not smiling; not now. He said; "I got your D.N.A. and I will destroy your reputation"! He held up a small baggie that looked to contain hair follicles. John looked at the hair and back to him and tried not to laugh. He held his breathe instead. He made a loud and exaggerated exhale and said; "O.K."; but I need some assurances. Lynchburg put the baggie back into his pocket. Johnathan teleported the baggie with his hair in it, to his kitchen trash can. Lynchburg did not know it was gone. What assurances do you need Mr. Spectrum; because I got you by the balls. First stop this mockery of a public trial by character assasination; and number two get the hell out of my house and respect my privacy. I am not asking for nothing that is out of your power and influence. John could tell the power and influence reference made Lynchburg's day. He smiled and said; "all right". He threw a satellite capable cell phone at him. John caught it. Lynchburg said; "you take orders directly from me, you understand"! John looked at Lynchburg walk around straighten his tie. He walked out as if he accomplished something he had the same mannerisms as that dummy assistant district attorney what's his name." Jones, and Shaggy walks out with him. The woman with the piercings lingered "You are incredible;" she said; "my name is Beatrice; if you open your mind to me I can help you deal with Lynchburg". John looked at her and said, "I don't need any help with Lynchburg". I intend to do what I am required to do and don't want any more problems." Beatrice, look at him I can't read your mind; but I can read your body language and your facial expression you are holding back an incredible secret." John looked at her after a long pause, said; "Madame you have a good day please don't come back." They left, and when they walked out of his front door, he continued to watch their egress on his security monitor. John took off his clothes and jumped into the shower.

Johnathan woke up the next morning and said; "Colonel, you there"? The Colonel said; "Of course I am, good morning." "Colonel, the C.I.A. Agent Lynchburg made contact with me yesterday;" John said. "Colonel did you find anything out about what is going on with my so-called legal problems. The Colonel said; "Yes, I would like to introduce you to

Natasha." Natasha's Icon voice was deep for a woman voice and she had a strong accent, John was not sure but it sounded like Russian. John said; "Ms. Natasha how are you". She said; "Good morning." I am the computer icon that has been programmed for espionage and counter espionage. She did not waste anytime on a formal introduction. "Mr. Spectrum you have been under surveillance and have been constantly followed by your government's agents ever since you were made aware of the feloons interest in your special abilities; every electronic device you own is under surveillance and your apartment loft is saturated with listening and recording devices. John was so angry he was fuming. "Please, go on." "Every person who you have has sex with, and associate with is subject to some type of eaves dropping." John was feeling his heart thump in his chest. "Colonel I cooperated what else I could do, my privacy means a lot to me this is the reason why I don't have an entourage or a bunch of body guards." The Colonel said; "Ms. Natasha is better suited to answer your question than I am". Natasha continued unperturbed by his interruption." We can enact every counter measure known to man, and we can deploy ones that are not known to man also." John's mood began to lighten; "What if they deploy electronic counter measure - counter measures. If they get an inkling of an idea that I am hip to them, being hip to me they will try something else." Natasha said; "We will teleport programming into you electronic devices to give them false images and information. We also defrag your systems of any virus or fail safes. If you have to go anywhere in private you can teleport there, the teleportation process creates no noise or light. We can enact these counter measures if you wish it. John said; "Yes, I wish it," very humbly. "Thank you Natasha." She said; "you're welcome". "If you don't require me any further I shall leave; and if you do require me again you can call me also. Good day, sir". John was relieved he went from being indignant and hostile to happy and content in a matter of seconds. "Colonel thank you, for your help, I got to train for a fight and I don't need any more headaches or distractions. John trained and trained for his upcoming heavy weight title defense and Lynchburg could not control his self. He looks at John as if John was a toy that he could play with and use at will. John put up with his childlessness.

Lynchburg was truly a child of privilege. He actually would shout and throw grown man temper tantrums. Johnathan meet with Agent Jones, Beatrice, and Agent Timothy Darth aka "Shaggy". He only met with them one time in the two week period before his title fight. He actually met and worked out with them. Shaggy was the strongest man in the world, literally, he could lift 10000 times his body weight; Sonya was a very powerful psychic. She was very weird and hard to talk to; because she knew everything. She literally did know everything she was using mind altering drugs to nullify her powers. Agent Jones was nothing special in the God given talent department, but his hand and eye coordination was beyond remarkable. He was and incredible marksman, and had no compassion for his fellow man.

He was a stone cold killer. John did not like being in his presence. He, was Lynchburg's personal assistant, where ever Lynchburg went he followed. He was sizing John up from the first time he saw him. John knew he was going to have a problem with him it was a matter of time. John kept close contact with General McCormick, and Capt. Tiffany Morgan. He felt they were down to earth and he could trust those two more than Lynchburg. He gave the General and Captain tickets to the fight and invited the two of them to fly there on his private jet, they both said; "Yes" of course. While they were in flight laughing and joking with one another, John's trainer knocked on the door. It was "D.J." John you got to see this; he did not say another word he walked in and turned the T.V. monitor on to the news.

Breaking news report scrolled across the screen in bold red letters. "Johnathan Spectrum accusations are false; that was the heading under the image of a press conference. The young lady Beatty Tomlin, who was doing the accusing, was in tears and was giving her side of the story. John looked at the TV and places his left hand on his forehead while he rested his elbow on his knee. The press conference was in absolute circus. She had a long drawn out story saying she was being manipulated coerced into making the accusation against John. She had a elaborate but also plausible explanation of why she did what she did; she was being blackmailed and she went so far as to apologize to Johnathan Spectrum and his fans. She left the podium, the Attorney for Beatty began to spin the crowd and media; a representative of the F.B.I. informed the news media that the charges against Mr. Spectrum have been dropped. Miss Coleman is not being charged and her story was credible and the F.B.I. is working with Miss

Coleman to bring the blackmailers which were unnamed to justice. The press conference ended in an uproar of media frenzy, screaming questions, yelling incoherent phrases it was absolute anarchy when D.J. cut the volume down. I am sorry for interrupting you; I thought you wanted to see that. The other people on the plane saw the same thing and they were cheering and applauding. The General said; "Well, you got to hand in to Lynchburg he did do what he said he was going to do." "That guy is something else, tell me about him"; John said. General McCormick and Capt. Tiffany Morgan looked at each other. D.J. saw the uneasiness and read the awkward silence in the jets cabin. He did not need a hint he left it alone on his own. The General said; "I don't know if we can speak here". John thought about what Natasha and the Colonel said about securing all his electronic devices from eavesdropping. "General I have some security prodicals in place you may talk freely;" John said. Capt. Morgan said; "Lynchburg is a man of privilege he grew up with a silver spoon in his mouth.

She went on he had an impressive résumé of Ivy League schools and references in the top positions in the government. "Wow", John said. "Wow he so childless and so insecure". The General raised an eyebrow. "Yes, that is my assessment of his disposition, "I am a professional athlete and I see that trait in a lot of the men I come in contact with in my career"; John said. John said; "I will be starting training camp a couple of months after this fight. If you could see some of the mindless behavior in the locker room you would be able to recognize it too." General McCormick made a slight smile and nodded his head. John received general calls from his friends and family congratulating him; he made a point to deflect questions about him paying her off and coercing her to change her testimony. John so-called friends went back to asking for money and favors from him and he did a professional 'spin job' on every person who called him including his agent. John's agent was upset and angry over several endorsements he lost in that 2 week media circus. He spoke to her and had to keep it short and sweet; he still had to maintain the perception of her working for him and not him working for her. The General said; "you now how to talk rings around people you should have been a politician". John laughed a little and shook his head. The plane touch downed at a private air field at John's request; because he wanted avoid the media circus that he knew was waiting on him at the airport. He changed his plans at the last moment; it gave him a little time before the rumor mill found out where he was. There were SUVs' waiting on them and not limos. John's trainers and staff stayed at the big casino hotel. The same luxury was afforded to the Captain, and General. John stayed at a Time Share condo he bought years ago through a dummy corporation. The town was all a buzz for anticipation of the fight and John was nervous! He felt he had a lot on his plate. He was a superstar athlete in boxing, and in football; now he is a government agent. Last but not least he was at the beckon call of extra-terrestrial that has evolved so high that it does not require a name.

'Fight Night;' John could not sleep the night before; because of his anxiety of his fight day. He spent the whole day lying in bed trying to relax. He turned off all his cell phones and sound equipment. When he got up he walked through his condo. When his trainers came and picked him up he was like a robot. He did not say a word his people were out side waiting on him in the stifling Nevada heat. John did not say a word he was actually meditating on how to knock his opponent out. His staff rode in vans and SUVs' they knew his fight routine they did not speak to him either. John made it through the coliseum he could hear the buzz of thousands of people. The noise, the laughing; he could feel the emotional energy of the spectators. He had a lot of extra security because of his recent allegations he was given the opportunity to skip the weight-in slash press conference, and was weighed-in without the hoopla and trash talking. He was ready, he was here, he no longer felt the anxiety, and his adrenaline was on full blast. John sat in the shower; of the locker room area he deliberately avoided the reporters and the news commentators.

The magic moment was now at hand. John heard the words, "let's go, its time", he got up and walked to the locker room door he could not hear his music, because the crowd was screaming and cheering. He walked into the arena and he had tunnel vision, his eyes were fixated on the ring and his opponent. John had this thing about not studying his fighting opponent he concentrated on himself and his fighting style and not the other guy. He felt that if he was at the top of his game, he could beat anyone. His opponent was there in front of him. He doesn't remember walking into the ring but, he was there. He was staring at another dude, who had a goofy look on his face. He was well muscled and new to the professional world of boxing; so he was hungry and passionate. John knew that this guy was the number one contender and he knew that his reputation could not suffer another blow if he ducked him. He had to fight the best or step down, he thought. Everything was a blur the introduction and the ref s last minute instructions and then; Ding! That was the last thing he heard when Bam! John was down on the mat! John could not believe it, he had to get up quickly, and he felt like he was moving in slow motion. John got to his feet very slow but he made it before being counted out. The ref. looked him in the eyes yelling over the crowds. "Look at me"; he said, "Can you continue"? John steady himself look the ref in the eyes and said; "You, damn right, I can continue!" The ref let Johns gloves go and step back quickly and said; "Fight!" The fighter 'J.J. Saturday Night', had a wide goofy smile on his face; and John was determined to knock it off. John let him have it, right, left, combos, and body shots. John went through his whole arsenal of boxing skills. J.J. Saturday Night was not smiling any more. John had to make up for being knocked down in the first round. The second round the third round, John knew through his fight experience that he scored more points than J.J. He also knew to win this fight he had to knock him out. That was John's primary goal. He had to play it smart. This guy was a rookie so-to-speak so John used one of the dirty tricks. It was legal as far as the rules went, but John wanted to make an extreme example of this guy. The fourth and fifth round came and went John won every round but the first. He threw combinations at J.J.'s chin and he concentrated on that one part of his face. Every time J.J.

threw and punch or combination John would hit him as hard as he could in this shoulders right were the socket met the arm. John noticed J.J. had trouble lifting both of his arms after the seventh round. John thought to himself, "Time to knock some sense into this dummies head!" John waited for it; he waited for it; J.J. threw a power punch trying to knock John out; and John beat him to the punch literally!

J.J. Saturday night was lying face first on top of the mat with his arse in the aid, completely 'out cold.' The arena erupted in cheers as the ref raised Johnathan's left glove in the air. He was the winner and he successfully defended his crown. John was happy and at the same timed subdued. He knew that the media - and his fickle fans would charge on him in a heartbeat. His trainers and his every one was in his corner, people whom he did not know were now in the ring, trying to shake his hand and pat him on the back. Johnathan was stopped for his post fight interview

This is interviewer; who was a former fight himself and was lucky enough to get a commentators gig, was waiting on John. As John approached him he put his left arm around Johns sweaty shoulders leaned in close as he stuck the micro-phone in his face. He turned his face toward the camera; "This is Chucky Dean, here with Johnathan Spectrum the now three-time heavy champion of the world. Chucky Dean turned to John, and said; "What was the first thing that went through your mind when you were knocked down. John was completely out of it, from the fight he was spent, his face was bruised and tender from the 'whooping'

J.J. gave him. John had to think before he spoke, his fan did not want to hear how embarrassed he was. John said; "I was impressed and ultimately surprised by J.J.'s hand speed." John did not answer the question. Chucky did not go any further he accepted the answer. Chucky said; "Would you give J.J. a second shot at the title. John had to spin Chucky; J.J. was a lot tougher than he thought. John said; "Nothing is ruled out, at this time, I would like to face another contender I am quite sure; there are others fighters waiting for a shot at the title too." I will eventually work my way back to J.J. Saturday night." Before Chucky Dean could say another word. John cut him off "Thank you", Chuck, I got to go; "John walked away to the locker room. John turned to D.J. and said; "Call ahead and have the cars waiting on us. I don't like these large crowds. As John took a towel off D.J.'s shoulder to wipe his face. He could not mistake the Imperial Japanese solider that was in the employ of the other 'fe-loon' was staring at him. John looked directly at him as the two warriors made eye contact the solider was gone in a blink of an eye. John rushed through the arena by passed the locker and shower. He also by-passed the gaggle of reporters and cameras, he got into the car. Captain Tiffany Morgan ran up to the S.U.V. window and knock on the window. When John let her in there was a renewed frenzy of camera flashes and more screaming questions. She step into the truck John slam the door shut and said; "Drive"! The driver was some guy D.J. hired and John did not know him. Take me back to my condo." Sir, we are going to leave the others; the driver said. John said; "They know where I am going; they will be fine."

"Capt. Morgan" John said; she responded "Tiffany." "Excuse me" John said; "Tiffany". Where's the General. The General went back to his hotel room with a couple of $500 dollars an hour escorts. "Oh"! John said, in a surprised reaction that he did not intend on being heard. Tiffany smirked and shook her head at him. "Well I am glad you found me"; he said. "I need to talk to you in private it can't wait for the night to conclude. Tiffany said; "What's so important". "It is concerning the recent trip I made". What the flight over from Detroit to Vegas;" she said. No not that trip the other trip, the long vacation I took that brought us together as acquaintances." She thought about it and said "Ooh"! That long trip. John was nodding slowly and said "Yeah"! Trying to keep his conversation as vague as possible for the sake of the driver, he did not know. John tipped the driver 50 bucks and said; thanks go back to the arena and wait for everyone else they are probably partying or something. He nodded got back into the truck and left. John walked into the modest condo, it was nice but it was not a super luxurious condo. John said; "I saw the solider; He noticed that the solider reference did not ring a bell." He had to explain, the Imperial Japanese solider that he had to fight to drive away the fe-loon. Then Tiffany said; "Oh"! long and slow. John looked at her, she was wasted." Captain Tiffany Morgan, I thought you had more discipline than that;" John said. She said, "I beg your pardon sir, I work hard and I play hard." Where's your bar, I still got some room in any tank for some more 'jet fuel.' John smiled in amusement. Everything is in the kitchen, be careful it is over the micro-wave," John said. Do you need any help? She said "No sir, I am a solider, if

I need your help I would ask for it." John said, OK., OK, as he put both his hands up in the universal sign to slow down. He watched her turn and go. John walked upstairs to the bedroom and took his clothes off and jumped into the shower John said; "Colonel are you there", Yes, I am always here; how may I help you. I saw the Japanese solider that was in the employ of the other fe-loon. The colonel said, "Are you positive." John could not help, but to hear concern in the computer icons voice, "Yes Sir, I am sure"; John said. The colonel said "Well this is a most interesting development". John said; "What does this mean". I could mean several things, the second fe-loon is going to try and recruit you for it-self as the fe-loon intend to seek revenge upon you for what you did on the other planet. Which that is highly unlikely, their race of species has evolved beyond revenge, love and petty emotions." "Well;" John said, 'What could it possibly be then?"

The colonel said, maybe he intends on taking you away from the fe-loons". "Taking me away like how." "Either trying to recruit like I said, or neutralizing you as a threat". John said; "Neutralize me, you mean killing me". The colonel said, "exactly." He knows who you are and where you live John, keep your guard up. That solider has the ability to teleport likes you do and have the same comparable combat skills. He is a solider from your second world war so he has a killer instinct that you don't have". "Thanks colonel for the warning;" John said. Colonel are their any more limitations on this teleportation ability." "Well, the colonel said; "There were a few; like we discussed and you over came one." John was curious which limitation was that." You no longer need to the teleportation apparatus to be physically worn on your person you have figured out that you can teleport things to you at will including the weapons in the arsenal. You only need to know where they are it does not have to be your line of sight. John was surprised I did know that was a limitation. The colonel said; "when the fe-loons first discovered the teleport technologies ions ago they where limited in such a way. You are a human with incredible survival instincts you have adapted overcame the fe-loon technology just after a short period of use. The fe-loons developed their talents after several thousand years. Our species human have the ability to grow, learn and evolve faster than any other sentient beings in the galaxy". John had no idea human beings had such an admirable quality of survival, and that other alien races envied us. The colonel continued, "This is the primary reason why the fe-loons have used our race as warriors and tried several times to covertly control your planet, and every single time we humans have detected and resisted and ultimately stopped any attempts of extra-terrestrial control or influence. John was very surprised, so this is the reason, or one of the reason for some much surveillance and concern by our government." The colonel said; "Yes." John said; "Thank you colonel; oh, by the way can I trust Capt. Morgan and General McCormick." The colonel said; "Yes they don't have any hidden motive they have been recruited by the fe-loon to be his two primary contacts on earth. They are the only two human beings on the planet that he has contacted. Now you are recruited by fe-loon you are now the third human being directly in contact with the fe-loon. Be careful who you let know that. Every nation who deploys any type of clandestine services knows who you are. John said; "I will do my best to not share any type of information that will jeopardize the country." The colonel said; "The world; you are your world's solider or champion only you can travel from planet to planet and stop crimes against humanity and other non-human beings. You were chosen specifically for the reason that your mind can not be read or dominated by psionics". "Wow talk about pressure," John said. John said, "Colonel may I talk to you later, I'm getting out of the shower now." The Colonel said; "Yes; and by the way Natasha has stopped several attempts I access your financial accounts, and your medical records. Your government want as much information as possible on you! John stop talking for a long while, and said colonel tell me I am secure. "You are secure" the colonel said. John let go a sigh of relief and said; "thanks and stepped out of the shower." John was deeply concerned as he wrapped a towel around his waist and step into his bedroom. There were no lights on in the bedroom the only illuminate came from the street lights outside and the bathroom, that was billowing steam from John's hot shower. Capt. Morgan was on his bed, on her hands and knees, with her back arched and facing the headboard. She had a very athletic body, she was well toned; she had a soldier's body. John was mesmerized by how sexy she looked. She looked at him and said; "To the victor goes the spoil." She arched her back in such a way; that her pussy and booty hole open at the same time. She said; "What are you waiting on, fall in private"! John did not think he reacted. Her open vagina was literally calling him. She was rolling her hips and arching her back in such a way that it looked like her lips were talking. He put his mouth on her pussy lips and kissed her with his warm tongue and wet mouth. John was on his hands and knees licking Tiffany Morgans swollen pussy. She was moaning in ecstasy; John pulled his mouth away to take a small breathe and to wipe away the excessive vaginal secretions. Tiffany grabbed him roughly by the ear. She turned to him, and with a look of sexual deviance said; "What the fuck are you doing, Eat my white asshole you black son of a bitch"! John said "O.K," scooped her up with both of his arms by her hips and thighs. He sat up right and pulled Tiffany sexy little body toward him. He buried his tongue inside her ass hole. Tiffany let out a high ohhh! But as John worked his tongue that ohhh, turned into a low humming noise. He knew he was doing something right. She did not say a word, or make any noises. Then John felt involuntary muscle contractions as she tensed up and then relaxed; as she relaxed her anus, John forced his tongue in, as she tensed up, her anal muscles clinched onto his tongue pulling his tongue into her further and further. John tongue was so far into her anus he was could not move it up and down any more. He slow pulled it out. Tiffany's body gave away her true feeling she shuddered and pulled her self out of Johns arms and then collapsed on the bed. She laid there as John was trying to catch his breathe. She opened his legs and said "round two," John was ready and he slowly pushed his 9½ inches into her 12am wetness. "Wow", John thought, "I very rarely have unprotected sex but this is great"! She let him have his way; for a woman who was used to giving orders she was very submissive. She did not complain or protest; whatever position

John turned her into she did it. She let him get on top of her and pound her as long and as hard as he wanted. Tiffany was laying in John's arms as John was giving it to her! She was covered in sweat; her mouth was half open from panting for air. Her eyes were glossed over as she stared into nothingness. She let John sire her multiple orgasms which in turn triggered so many endorphins that she was in a state of euphoria. John pulled out at the last moment, and blasted his cum onto her stomach as Tiffany laid there in a sexual trance. He looked at her as he collapsed next to her completely out of energy. She was laying on her back and first only turned her eyes to meet him then she turned her head. They were both laying there face to face on there backs looking into one anothers eyes as if they just meet for the first time. John smiled at her, and put one of his arms around her and she rolled over on top of him, she put her head on his chest and he held her while he went to sleep. They slept all night and morning; John woke up around 3 o'clock that afternoon. Tiffany was gone; John began to wonder was that a dream. He rolled over and felt the wet spot on the bed and said; "I guess not." He was laying there trying to recall the details of last night and he heard a phone ringing. It was not his phone; he did not recognized this ring tone; it kept ringing so he looked for it. It was that satellite phone that Agent Lynchberg gave him. After going through his unpacked luggage he found it and answered it. "Hello," John said, the voice on the other end said; "how are you I am Agent Lynchberg are". John thought about it; "I know Lynchberg, you dont sound like him." Lynchberg sir, is your primary contact person. "I am your primary contact; so I am

Lynchberg"! John said; "O.K. how may I be of services sir",? We need you right away, there is a carrier battle group off the Coast of California there is a helicopter in route, Mr. Spectrum it is imperative you get on the helo, you will be briefed when you get here. Lynchberg out"! The call ended abruptly, John rushed to put on his clothes, he grabbed several pieces of his luggage that was unpacked, he thought to himself so much for staying for a couple days. "Colonel," John said; "I have been called, and I don't know why, I am being transported out to a carrier battle group. What were the teleportation limitations again? The colonel said the limitations are basically you. You can not go where you have not been, and you can not will something to you, you never known existed or cannot see; but your teleportation ability are unique only to you and you alone. The colonel said, "do you know what the details are?" Johnathan said; "no," I will be briefed when I get there. The colonel said; fair enough tell me about your mission and your mission details when you can." The colonel said; "I can hear the helicopter approaching your condo." John was surprised because he did not hear the chopper blades until they were on top of him. John grabbed his bags and headed for the door. The colonel said; "contact me when you are done." John said; "O.K." Then as John turned and locked the condo of his front door he saw D.J. laying on his front porch in the Nevada heat in a drunken hangover. John picked him up and left him on his couch; "Hey, D.J., hey D.J.," wake up!" John said. D.J. could barely open his eyes, but he did. John said; "Tell everybody that I went on vacation, I am going to be gone for a week or two." John did not know actually how long but a week or two sounded good. He ran back to the door and closed it. The helicopter was landed on the street and there was a man in a flight suit walking toward John's condo. The pilot said; Mr. Spectrum I presume; I am Lt. Cortez, may I help you with your bags. John said; "Thanks", and handed him his smallest bag and took his large suitcases himself. They moved quickly the helicopter that was in the middle of the street and it was holding up traffic. The helicopter was aloft before John had his safety belt fastened and the door was closed. The view from the halo was impressive the copter was low enough to see the details of Las Vegas. He heard his cell phone over the copter blades. It was Capt. Morgan to John surprise, "what's up;" John said, Capt. Morgan paused and maintain her professional military bearing. She addresses Johnathan with Mister. She said; Mr. Spectrum you are being summoned to a briefing that requires your expertise," John was a little annoyed by her lack of friendliness. He said; "Yes, ma'am any thing else"? Tiffany voice soften significantly and said; "No"! When will I get to coordinate our actions with you and the General;" John said? Capt. Morgan said, "you are under the directions of the "Company" now. This is no longer our responsibility." John said; "do you have anything to give me, on who, what, when, where." She said; "No," I just wanted to thank you for the nice trip I had a lot of fun and so did the General." John said; "No problem, when will I get to see you again"? Mr. Spectrum this is an unsecure line;" Capt. Morgan Out"! That explains why she was so stand offish. Well I hope the precautions that I made with the colonel and Natasha pays off. John thought to himself. The trip was uneventful it took a little time to fly from Nevada to 200 miles off the west

coast of California to a assault carrier battle group. When John touched

down he could see the usual suspects on the flight deck waiting for him.

"Shaggy", Agent Jones, and the old woman. There was a man there that

John never seen before. He was assuming that he was the other Lynchberg.

He got off the helicopter and the Navy personnel immediately relieved him

of his travel gear and took his bags to his cabin. The group did not say a

word when they met up, the flight deck was loud of course. The C.I.A

agent Lynchberg led them to a top secret briefing room. When they went

through the secure areas and sat down. Lynchberg did not waste any time.

He introduced himself as Lynchberg, he was tall with red, hair, freckles,

and green eyes he was thin and well muscled. He said; you are being

pressed into service, and needless to say, you already know this will be the

first action you will be taking with Mr. Spectrum. The others looked at

John with a look of loathing and apprehension. John was glad they could

not read his mind. If they knew how he felt he would probably have a fight

on his hands. John pretended to not notice them but the old woman just

continued to stare at him. Lynchberg went on. He said; "I few days ago we

intercepted this cube. As he spoke the lights went dim and a projection of

a cube appear on the wall. John could not help to notice the dead bodies

in the room laying around the soul survivor. He was an African, John

could not tell what region, but he could tell this by his strong ethnic

features and accent. The soldiers who appeared to be black Ops. Went

through the room in a hurried pace, ignoring the cube that was in plan sight. As they gather intelligence one of them place a weapon on the table were the cube was; one of the special operation soldiers said; "Hey what is this?" More to himself than to the others in the room. The cube shift into a different contour, and it projected a hologram into the room. The soldiers were startled as the holograph projected out into the open air above the table. The projection shows, what appear to be gold bricks. And what appeared to be aliens in some type of survival suits. As the holographic projection proceeded you can see the aliens begin to make forward moving motions, to what appeared to be soldiers, they were dressed in rags, they did not appear to be professional. The cube was thrusted in to the soldiers hands as the cube then projected images, of that solider bathing with women of all different races and he was surrounded by gold bricks as his holographic projection smiled back at that very surprised solider. The holograph show him nodding in acceptance as he made a motion with his right hand. There was a cold shiver of shock and anger that went through John. He was watching in absolute horror as a gaggle of little children, were ushered to the alien in armor. The children were crying, and in shocked and they walked toward the armored clad alien, as if they were people being led to the electric chair. The cube showed the transaction take place for every child the solider was given a gold brick. The alien reached out to grab the rope that bond the children together, you could see the horrid silent screaming John turned away, he could not take it any more. That was not the end of it. It went further, to computer generated icons of females and children. The computer icon counted out to be 200 hundred woman and 800 hundred children male and female

The last thing that the cube projected was a date, and longitude and latitude. The projection ended with Lynchberg grim face looking at John, as if he was the perpetrator of the obvious human rights crime. "Now, lady and gent's, this is what we believe, that this cube was solely a device to communicate with. It showed the humans that were so foolish enough to take this device what to do and where to meet them for another human transaction. The prisoner of that special ops team said he was very valuable." He did not hold up well under vigorous interrogation." There was a broad smile that ran cross Agent Jones face, John knew he meant torture. John was thinking to himself; "what the hell did I get my self into." Lynchberg said; "the professionals at Langley cannot communicate or use the cube. The cube just projects the same images over and over again. You have ten days to get ready, you are going to be dropped in, and you are to killed, the human traitors, who are selling humans to aliens. You are to capture the aliens who think we are cattle to be bought and sold. You are also required to gather as much intelligence as possible on these extra-terrestrial. Lynchberg said; "any questions?" Who are the soldiers and what country are they in. They are from West Africa. They represent themselves as freedom fighters but they are raping and murdering, and engaging in human trafficking. "The have just started or more likely we are just made aware that so-called freedom fighting rebel army is selling humans to aliens off planet. We have no idea what is going on, we don't know where they are going nor Why they need humans. "Mr. Spectrum"; every eye tuned on Johnathan." You are the only human here who had actual contact with another alien race, 'could you please enlighten us. John said; "I don't know"! Special Agent Jones said; "why do we need this guy, he ain't nobody"! The old woman piped up; "we need him more than you know"! Shaggy sat there looking from face to face unmoved one way or the other. Before Agent Jones could say anything; he open his mouth in a rebuttal; but it snapped closed. You could tell by his rapid eye movements from John to the old woman, it was not voluntary. Agent Jones tries to get up, he was doubly embarrassed when he could only sit there. Then Lynchberg looked at the old lady, with her leather jacket and piercing and did not say a word. Lynchberg said "lady and gent's," that's it we got thirty days to steam to the coast of Africa, and stop this wholesale of humans. We will be there in ten days you have training to do Mr. Spectrum. Lady and gentlemen you are dismissed. John walked out of the room, and avoided Agent Jones eye contact. He was so angry that he had sweat on his brow and was breathing as if he was out of breath from running. The old woman evidently released him because he stalked out of the room. John walked out and looked a Shaggy who sat there with the old woman. Lynchberg said; "Mr. Spectrum, one word." Lynchberg on the new Lynchberg said; "do have any ideas of what might be going on"? John said; "I really don't know, I'll only be guessing." I read your report," Lynchberg said. I was very interested about the parts were you mention the hybrids you were fighting and the waste disposal area, for human's. John looked him in the eyes, the waste disposal area. John encounter still haunted him. He never mentioned it and he did everything he could to hide the fact. He knew Lynchberg read his facial expressions and his body language. So Lynchberg let the subject rest. The trip was very eventful, John and Agent Jones, could not help but to get on each others nerves. Agent Jones went out of his way to try and embarass or show up John when ever and how ever he could. It pissed off Agent Jones more when he could not. He was equally peeved when the members of the crew were asking Johnathan Spectrum for his autograph. He was fuming every time he spoke to one of the female members of the crew. John trained with the different type of weapons on the ship; he began to like his M-4 Carbine as he became more and more proficient at it. John noticed that Shaggy and the old woman were never apart. They were inseparable. He did not think anything about it.

The ship and the battle group was off the coast of East Africa. The four of them the old woman Shaggy, Agent Jones and Johnathan Spectrum were given last minute instructions. On how to infiltrate and how to exfiltrate. They all entered the countries in different ways and had twenty days to get to the so-called transaction point. John enters the country via fishing boat he left all of his valuables on the ship, he wore a disguise which the others thought was ridiculous; but he had a plan a ball cap, and shades. If someone recognized him he would deny it, teleport somewhere public make a personal appearance to create an alibi that can not be disputed and teleport back. He thought how convenient it was to be able to do so. While he was on the ship he locked himself in his cabin and would teleport back to his condo in Vegas. He left that part out of his briefing, When he initially spoke, to the National Security Advisor, and the Director of the C.I.A.. The colonel told him the only limitations he had were the one he put on himself. John was beginning to understand. He could not will himself to teleport to some where he has never been. Once he has been there, he can teleport back and forth at will 'so the sky was the limit.' John did not know how well that would sit with the government agencies interested in his new found abilities.

When he finally made it to the coast of Africa, he tried his best to fit in but, he did stuck out like a sore thumb. The Africans knew he was different right away and the blending in with the locals was out of the question. He tried to act as a tourist to their continent. He did not go to any clubs or any resorts he made the long arduous journey from East, to West Africa from truck to camel to train. It was not as easy as he initially thought. He came across a small village and decided to stay there for the night. He walked around the village and was just as curious about the villagers and the village as they were about him. He was taken aback, by the poverty that he has seen throughout his trip, and was afraid to take any thing from them or ask for anything. John went back to the truck and saw that his things that were locked up were takened

He was angry and at the same timed saddened. He was ashamed that he made $ 250 million dollars a year and was angry over a bag of missing potato chips and a box of M.R.E., John was going to teleport back to Vegas but decided against it, if he left his truck it would probably not be there when he teleported back. So John took the lead of the villagers and went to sleep when the sun went down. It made a lot of sense he thought if you don't have electricity why would you be up all night. So he tried to sleep but the heat was oppressive. He was laying there trying to concentrate to fall asleep when he heard screaming. It was a loud shriek! That sharp sound broke his concentration he poke his head out of the truck and was immediately greeted with an AK47 assault rifle pointed toward him. He looked at the gun man, and was drawn to his eyes. The gun man eyes was glazed over with a blank stare; he was high on something. John was pulled roughly out of the back of the truck. He was now surrounded by gun men, who had that same look of intoxication on their faces also. John's attention was drawn away from the gun men. The others were pulling women and little girls out into the villages center by their hair kicking and screaming. John was struck in the stomach by one of the gun men, he had on mirror shades, a light blue U.N. peace keepers beret, and a bullet proof vest, that looked like it had a bullet stuck in it. The gun man said "Look at me, look at me." In broken English. "Who are you"? He looked the man in the face and into his mirror shades and did not say a word. The head gun man motioned for the others to restrain John. John was in a state of shock he could not believe that this was going on. He was being punched in the stomach and face as they held he up. He was punched back into reality as he watched a group of gun men pull down a ten year old girl and began to mount her. John said; "I am a real man, that's who the fuck I am"! He teleported out of the two gun men's hands that were holding him he was standing over the wanna-be rapist; he had his loin cloth down and was 1 second away from penetration when John, grabbed him by the neck and pulled him off the little girl. Now it was their turned to be in shock. John forcefully turned him around into a head lock. Tighten in arm and fore arm around his naked neck. He picked the gun man up off of his feet as he broke his neck. John teleported from gunman to gun man he shot them with there own guns and slashed and hacked them with their own machete's. The man with the mirror shades, was not a professional he was a god cursed coward he started spraying the whole area as John teleported in and out existence at will. He did not know like others that his will to teleport was faster than a speeding bullet. The cowardly gun man sprayed the area with assault rifle bullets he was hitting and killing his own gunmen. The cowardly gun man expended his magazine and went to reload as he looked down to get another magazine John appeared in front of him instantaneously; looked him in the eyes and punched him like he punched 'J.J. Saturday Night'! The mirror shades broke and cut his face, and he fell where he stood like a sack of dirty laundry. The villagers were crying and in shock, and so was John. He looked at movies and watched cable news, and had no idea how bad these so-call war lords and gangs were. He tried to help the villagers but they were just as afraid of him as they were the gun men. The few people who were in hiding and who actually ran away came back as the shooting stopped, helped John with the villager. The villagers started stripping the gun men. They started to exact revenge on the gun man who were wounded and left lying there bleeding. John walk over to the head gun man, and looked down at him. He examined him very closely, he was wearing two gold watches, gold chains gold and silver rings on all of his fingers he was thin, but appeared to be in good health compared to the others. John strip of all of his weapons and went through his pockets. He found a satellite cell phone, similar to Johns phone. John raised an eyebrow because he thought that was interesting. He found a wad of cash, on him, he had a one thousand dollar bill, and a bunch of 100 dollar bills rolled up underneath him. John said out loud; "Who here speaks English?" The little girl that he saved from being raped said; "I do." John was silent and then spoke to her. "Come here beautiful;" he said. She was afraid, and stood there motion less. John said; "don't be afraid, I won't let him hurt you". The little girl walked over to him. John said; "Sweetie, could you find me some rope, or something I can tie him up with," as he nodded toward the head gunman. She nodded and ran off and brought back some wire that you use to make fences for cattle or stock. John looked at the wire, looked at the head gunman, he decided that's good enough for him. He twisted that wire around his biceps and arms, round his wrist while his hands were behind his back. He also bound his thighs, lower legs and ankles. John told the little girl; let me speak to your elders. She went and got an old man who could barely walk, and a blind old woman. They said; "thank you," the little girl said as she translated what the village elders said. John said, he wanted to apologize about what happened, I think they came here to rob me he said, "I am a stranger in your land." The male elder said; "No they did not come here for you, they came her for us". The little girl translated the conversation. "They were here to rob you"; John asked, "No, they are the soul snatchers they are here to steal our women and children, and sell their souls to the devil." John thought about and put two and two together. This was an incredible coincidence that he would run into the men who was affiliated with the group of unidentified soldiers selling humans to aliens. John said; "Who are they, what do you call them. The girl translated, the elder said; "We call them the soul stealers." Can you tell me anything about them, no matter how small the detail. The little girl had a lot of information to give to John. John sat there and listened to it all. The so-called transaction spot was two days away in another country. I would not think that Lynchberg would care; as long as we maintain our primary mission that would not be his problem. He heard the head gun man come to; he started threatening the villagers. He could barely move because the wire that John tied him up with was cutting off his circulation. He was scaring the little girl so badly she was in tears. He look at her and said; "what is your name?" she said; "Nadjha;" "beautiful he would never hurt you or your village again". She looked up at him with her little brown eyes, and nodded. John said; "I will be back." He walked over and kicked the head gun man in his nuts, picked him up threw him over his shoulder. Johnathan teleported his satellite phone to his left hand and called Lynchberg. Lynchberg said, "What's so important that you have to break radio silence"? I got some new information for you I have another player in this illegal enterprise we were tasked to investigate." Lynchberg was silent and said; "I can't get him out of there, the time table will not be altered. The mission parameters are still a go. Mr. Spectrum I need not remind you, that you are one of MY assets on the ground." John cut him off; he was beginning to sound like the other Lynchberg. "I am coming to you, the time table is still in play." He hung up his satellite phone. He repeated to him self; "the time table is still no play," I am starting to talk like a C.I.A. spook." John instantaneously teleported back to the assault carrier. He rematerialized on the flight deck in the middle of the night, with the gun man thrown over his shoulder. The watch stander screamed in alarm, intruder, intruder, the ship immediately went to general quarters as an armed company of marines backed up by sailors approached him with there weapons drawn and at the ready. They could be seen visibly relaxing as they recognized Johnathan Spectrum. Lynchberg ran out on the deck and was just as surprised to see John as the others. He looked around and said; "Mr. Spectrum this is a top secret mission as soon he got into ear shot to whisper." Lynchberg and the other unnamed C.I.A. stooges led him and his captive below decks for a de briefing.

The gang of agents, and security personnel went straight for the secure area of the ship. Lynchberg held his peace until then. As soon as the unauthorized people was outside of the secure bulk head doors Lynchberg rounded on Johnathan and said, "What! do you think this is a circus."?

Who the hell is this and why are you not where you are suppose to be. Lynchberg walks over to the gun man and said hey, in 4 different African dialects until he found the one that he can communicate with this gun man with.

As Lynchberg spoke to him the more he was interest-in what he had to say. Lynchberg body language change from hostile to normal. He spoke to him in length until Lynchberg slowed him a computer generated picture of the cubes holographic images. The head gunman recognized him self in the images, he quickly shut his trap, as you can see fear roll across his smug face. Lynchberg asked him a question; no answer, then he appeared to asking the same question over and over again. Lynchberg stopped questioning him, and said; "I can loosen your binds so you can relax." He started tapping him on his chest. Lynchberg looked him up and down turned him around and looked at his hands as they were beginning to turn purple from the lack of circulation. Lynchberg said; "I can loosen your binds." "I know that you understand me, Tundé." John was surprised at how in just short of time Lynchberg found his name a knew that he spoke English. Tunde spoke this time and he sound defeated; "Please loosen them I can not feel my hands. Lynchberg pulled out a Swiss army knife, and unfolded the pliers/wire cutters. The moment before he cut the wire around his hands he said; "Tell me what I want to know". Tunde, was out done; he was anticipating pain relief and was asked a simple question for his suffering to end. He was working it through in his head, he said; "Yes, anything." "Where is this alien landing point"; said Lynchberg.

Lynchberg; to his credit did not relent. The alien landing point was were the original intelligence from the cube said it was. Lynchberg clipped the wire binding his wrist. John looked at his hands and was feeling guilty for tying the wire so tight. It was working out to their advantage. Tunde told him every thing as Lynchberg clip wire after wire. The wire was digging into his skin and it looked painful. After the interrogation there was a pile of bloody wire lying on the floor in front of a very daze and confused gun man. He confirmed every thing that little Nadjha said; Where it was, exactly how many women and kids it were, how many men they had working for them. The one thing that stood out the most was there initial contact was a Japanese man who did not speak much. He described them and John had a strong suspicion that it was same Japanese solider in the employ of the other fe-lon. John walked out of the room with Lynchberg and said; "So where do we go from here"? Lynchberg turned on John with fighter reflexes and said; "Leave the spying for the professionals, sir"! "You have a mission, and you are not to deviate from the mission parameters again"! I want a detail account of the teleportation phenomenon that you are entrusted with. You are a very deceitful individual Mr. Spectrum, you neglected to tell us that your teleportation had such a long range". "I did give you a detail account of my abilities, this talent that was bestow upon me, is new to me too I am learning it as I go along", John said in just as rude a tone as Lynchberg. Lynchberg soften a little and said; You are now an asset of the C.I.A. You heed to be debriefed and given proper training on how to use your new abilities. We can put you through some trails and experiment... Before Lynchberg said another word John said; "Experiment on who?!" Lynchberg looked surprised as if he let the cat out of the bag.

Lynchberg started to back pedal and tap dance;" No, no, that's not what I meant. John yelled "Fuck off"! I know what you meant "You want me to work with you I will; but I am not your asset."! John teleported out of the carrier battle group, and back to the village. John told the villagers that he was there to help them when they saw him appear out of nothingness. The villagers noticeably relaxed as they watch little Nadjha run up to him and jump into his arms. "Nadjha, what happen while I was away"? John was distance as he thought about the verbal exchange he had with Lynchberg. She was talking and did not know it. He was pulled back to the present by Nadjha, who was pulling on his arm as he spoke. John was so out of it. Nadjha's family was all there smiling at him as he shook there hands. Hi, John said; "Please forgive me I am distracted, how are you doing"? Nadjha family was overbearing in their thanking him He could not help but to feel surprised and embarrassed as Nadjha father ask, him to marry her. Johnathan Spectrum politely declined, and tried to walk back to the truck he left he still had to try and get some sleep before his mission come ahead. Johnathan could not shake them, he finally asked them if any of them wanted to take him to the warlord's compound. They all abruptly stopped talking and the all had an excuse why they could not make it. John watch as the hesitantly walked away. John walked back to his truck and noticed that his bag of potato chips and his box of M.R.E's had returned. He did actually get some sleep, he woke up and saw that the bodies from the night before were still there lying where they were had stripped them naked. John called Nadjha; as she walked up he asked her why have they not been buried those bodies. She said; "They don't deserve it, they are refuse". "There is no argument from me on that". John said; "Where are your elders I would like to speak to them again. "They are there"; Nadjha said. John walks over to the largest hut in the village the old man was wearing every piece of gold jewelry they found on the dead gun men. His hut was large and that was were they stored all of the newly obtained rifles, pistols and R.P.G's and ammo. John could not help but to see how arrogant the elder has become now that he had a gun in his lap. John said, could you bury those bodies, and have one of your men show me were the rebel's stronghold is. The elder's tone of voice remarkably change to, he no longer sounded like a scared old man John meet the day before. The old man said; "Why should I, they don't matter to me?" "I don't care". "The other warlord will find out what happened here and will want revenge." The elder said; "let him come we have guns, trucks and bullets. I am not afraid. John said, "What about the animals wondering into the village trying to eat them." The elder said; "We have guns to protect ourselves let the hyenas eat." "What about the diseases that will fester in those bodies. You can not protect your self from diseases with bullets;" John said. The elder said; "It will be done, I have to find men that will work for strangers for free". John said don't worry I will pay, you a thousand dollars and I will give each of you a 100 hundred dollars for working. The elder said; "Oh," as his eyes got wide. I will make sure it is done tomorrow. John said; "I will not be here tomorrow, I have a pressing engagement that I can not miss. Do it today or I will leave you alone, with disease and no money." The elder said; "It will be done," John unrolled the $1000 dollars bill off the wad of cash that he found on Tunde; and gave it to the elder. John gave each villager $100 dollars he did not have time to wait so he left them and hope they did the right thing. He was deeply trouble; that he inadvertently created another warlord. He said goodbye to Nadjha, and boarded his truck and left the village. The satellite cell phone started ringing he looked at his satellite phone forgot that he still had Tunde's phone in his pocket. He reached into his pocket, and he open it up to a text. The text was in French and John could not read it. He drove all day to the so-called rendezvous. There they were meet by another Lynchberg he was a black man with a strong African features, and spoke like he was a Harvard graduate. The third Lynchberg looked over the motley crew of misfits, an agent that look, like a agent he wore shades, and vest, and denim blue jeans. The old woman was wearing a white tank top, that was so sheer that you can see her old weather beaten skin and dried up titties.

John had on a fresh change of clothes and smelled like soap because he teleported home and took a bath. He was being examined by Lynchberg III because he most certainly have been debriefed by Lynchberg II. Then Shaggy, who was there at the old woman side he was wearing a tank top blue jeans like she was. John thought they were odd; but Lynchberg III did not give them the same scrutiny as he was given. I guess he was use to working with them. Lynchberg said; "We have to wait till the aliens make contact we have an agent inside their organization. We go when he give us a signal, now lady and gentlemen, we have troops to back you up. We want and we need these aliens to be taken alive". Agent Lynchberg III looked at Agent Jones and said; "Alive"! Agent Jones did not make eye contact and said; "Alright, I heard you." The area of contact was a semi-arid area. It had small trees some grass, you can see a person come at them miles away. Lynchberg III turned to John and said, "Mr. Spectrum this is were you come in." You are to make first contact, you can teleport there I am told without any difficulties." That was more of a question than a statement. John said; "Yes", Lynchberg III said; "Good. Know that you are the 'Lynch pin', of this operation. Your surprising them will give us ample time to cross the sierra and closed the trap any questions"? No one answered he said; "good; Lets go and take up position." John said; "Lynchberg," as Lynchberg III began to walk away. Lynchberg III turned on him with the same rattle snake reflexes as the other Lynchberg. John put both his hands up in the universal sign of surrender. Lynchberg III could not hide his frustration and said; "Yes," in a very course manner. John took the satellite cell phone out of his pocket and show Lynchberg III the text in French. "Could you please translate this for me;" John said. 'White Lily', football field tomorrow at any time! John said; "Thanks," and he looked at Lynchberg III and said; "I did not know they played football in Africa"? Lynchberg said; "They play soccer." 'White lily football arena is in East Africa a few hundred miles away". Was there something that was important there they requires my attention"? John thought about it and said "No". Lynchberg III tossed the satellite phone back at John who made a clumsy catch it and watch Lynchberg walk away.

It was the same old shit different day. They hurried up to get into their hiding positions and waited. They waited all day long. John was bored out of his mind, and did not teleport back to his condo in Vegas because he did not want to arouse suspicion. Lynchberg said; "Game On"! As he look at a lap top that gave him a real time satellite feed of what was going on around them. John looked out at the horizon and could barely see the trucks with the naked eye. The dust trail was his best indicator that some one was on the horizon. "Mr. Spectrum get ready;" Lynchberg III said. John said; "Colonel;" "Yes", the colonel said. I am about to go into action I need several things." The Colonel said; "at your service." "I need full body armor could you teleport it to me as teleport into action. The colonel said; Yes, I will teleport it onto you 1 millisecond after you materialize. Now Mr. Spectrum the question is what type of body armor do you want. Remember we have at our disposal every weapon conceived by human beings. Could you send me something that is experimental, but at the same time works. I don't want to be looking stupid literally and figuratively. The colonel said "O ye of little faith." Human beings have progressed quit significantly sense I was fighting," The colonel said." John had to concede to his point. "Thank you, colonel for your help please be ready I will tell you, when." John said. The colonel said; "Good luck"! John went to it with his palms sweating and he noticed that the old woman was looking at him. That old woman was creeping me out John thought. Lynchberg said; "Now"! John so distracted by the old lady that he did not hear it. "Hey dummy"! John looked at him. "Yeah, you, now"! Lynchberg III said. John look at the horizon where he saw the dust settling he willed himself across the sierra to the horizon and communicated his request for body armor to the colonel via his will. John reappeared in the middle of the trucks as they were array to protect the human cargo. John was wearing a armor plated exo-skeleton It was flat black in color it had pockets of Kevlar, and steel plate and ballistic fabric in all the right places. John was incased, head to toe in armor the helmet did not give away his facial features it was squared off around his face, the face plate was polarized so the brilliant sun light did not foul his vision. The face plate had a smart link to the hybrid M4 Carloine that was teleported to John with the suit. He surprised every human there, and the aliens that were standing there too, but they could not be seen by our radar, only by the naked eye.

John got the element of surprise and went to work. He started first by shooting all the drivers in every truck. The smart gun target display would illuminate green when a target is acquired. Orange when the target is not in gun range, red when the target was out of range. Yellow when the target was a friend, and then black when the target that was acquired was effectively neutralized. John teleported in range, out of range, left right on top of truck hoods and roofs. He was all over the place literally. He would fire three round burst into the war lords minions. Blood, guts, shit, vomit was all over the ground it was gruesome. John did not noticed the arrival of the others the old woman was levitating in air with her legs crossed onto one another her hair was floating and swirling around her in an eerie unnatural way. John saw that and was so in awe, that got him shot in his stomach by a solider that was crouching under one the trucks. Shaggy picked up the truck with one hand, tossed it over. The old woman who eyes where all white looked at him; and he screamed in pain as his arms were broken and folded up like a piece of note book paper! John had to recollect himself the bullet did not go through the armor; but the inertia made him double over in pain and take a knee. It was over as quickly as it started. John on one knee scanned to whole area. The old woman was levitating, Shaggy was standing there as close to her as possible Agent Jones was suspended in the air in such a contorted position. He looks like he was there against his will. The aliens had him up in some type of suspensor field. Agent Jones was in the field, with only bullet and rocket propelled grenade shoot at them. John could also hear F-22 fighter jets over head. Lynchberg III did a good job springing this trap. The aliens were surrounded on the ground by ground troops and covered by fighter jets. Contact with the aliens were the goal here, not saving the humans, John just realized! John stood up as he favored his stomach. The aliens body language gave every one on the ground the indication that they were looking at John. The alien that was standing in the middle pointed at John. Every body there turned at John. John stood there with his shoulders hunched and said; "What"?

The alien motioned for John to come closer, John lower his M-4 carbine and walked toward them. "We will speak to you"! The alien said; "I am not reading any malice in your thoughts, your mind is blank to me." What are your intentions. My intentions here was to save the humans from unknown and perceived danger". John said. John choose his words carefully; he did not know the truth behind their action. John willed him self to teleport his weapon and body armor away; "We are humans and we react very badly out of fear, what are your intentions with us"? As John stood there the suspensor field that held Agent Jones in placed dropped him. The bullets that was fired at the aliens fell to the ground. The grenade that was fired at them exploded inside the suspensor field and the shrapnel fell harmlessly to the ground. John stood their as the alien approached, Lynchberg III stood up and stood next to John, his weapon at the ready, the alien stopped John said to Lynchberg; "Lower your weapon" in a low tone. "Try and appear unthreatening to them." Lynchberg III relented and lower his weapon. The alien said, that human standing next to you is very angry, we don't want to par lee with him. John turned to Lynchberg III and said; "they only want to speak to me." Lynchberg III said; "Who the hell are you, I don't know you, I can not allow it." The alien said, "fear, anger, malice, hatred, your mind is open to us we will not speak to you". Lynchberg III anger was showing in his facial expression and he went out of his way to try and hide it. Lynchberg turned to John an said in a very low and belligerent tone we are going to have words after this is over. "You tell them that; we want to know why they are on our planet! Who are they, and what can they do for us." John said; "you know they can hear you as well as read your mind this is the reason why they don't want to talk to you." Before Lynchberg can verbalize a rebuttal." A group of men and women landed via helicopter. The group of men and women, walked by everyone else as if they weren't there and tried to speak to the aliens. Lynchberg said; "What is this"? A woman who was much older than either of them turned to Lynchberg and said; "You are relieved report back to your field commander for debriefing." Lynchberg III turned and walked away from John, giving him a look that a child would give another child that has tattled on him. The soldiers that were with them started releasing the human cargo, and ushering them to different trucks, to be taken out of the area, possibly to an aid station. Every thing was taken the trucks the bodies, and to John surprise the survivors. The bullets the weapons everything. John was standing there as if he was a innocent bystander watching it all. The men in women who relieved the initial contact team were talking to the aliens to some great length.

Johnathan Spectrum was relieved that he did not have to do it. It just was one more thing, to worry about he thought. Lynchberg II called John on the satellite phone returned to the carrier, for debriefing Shaggy, Agent Jones, and the old woman knew the routine the left and they all went their separate ways. Johnathan thought about teleporting back, but did not want to deal with Lynchberg II any longer than he had to. John decided on driving back. Tundé cash came in handy. Tundé had over twelve thousand dollars rolled up in $100 hundred dollar bills in his pocket. John stayed in really nice hotels, ate well and tipped excessively. John also took his time for another reason. He had a date at the White Lily football field, and was curious as to who sent them the text. He drove across the border, and made to East Africa. He stayed in the White Lily Hotel across from the White Lily Sports Arena. John checked himself into the hotel took a long hot bath and ate a steak dinner. John asked the waiter as he came to his table, "was that the White Lily football field, across the road?" He said; "Yes sir, It is the very one". The waiter went so far as the describe, it as if he was selling it. He said it can seat 10,000 spectators it is the most modern and luxurious stadium in all of Africa. It has sky boxes, and jumbotron score board, it is a modern marvel it rivals the stadiums in Europe and North America for its architecture John looked at him with an appreciative smile, and said; "Thanks." He tipped the waiter at $100 dollar bill. The waiter nodded and bowed several times and cleared the table and left. John went to his room and looked out of suites, balcony doors at the sports arena. As he did so he could see a lone figure standing in the middle of the soccer field. The distance was so far away he could not make out details of the person. John thought to himself, maybe that's my blind date. He willed himself to teleport to the arena's playing field. John was surprised but, at the same time he should have known better. It was the Japanese solider, that was in the employ of the other fe-loon. The solider stood there he had murder in his eyes. He said in a very strong accented voice; "we have some unfinished business. I have never been defeated in single combat," John raised an eyebrow; "There is a first time for everything." The Japanese solider jumped in the air and kicked John in the mouth with a round house kick. John reeled and place his hand over his bloody mouth. He spat out blood, and could feel that one of his teeth was loose. John took a knee the Japanese solider went in to a flurry of karate strikes and kicks. John was caught off guard by his intensity and by the randomness of his teleporting. Johnathan was out done, this guy was not underestimating him. John had to do the same in order to survive

John teleport away from each attack. The solider came at him John would teleport out his striking range. The two of them did this for an hour they were both sweating in the African heat. Neither man was going to back down or leave. The solider said to John; "fight me"! John said; "O.K," and punched him the face with a 'hay maker'. It was the soldiers turn to reel back and take a knee to recover from a stunning blow. John took the opportunity to take a breather himself. The solider recovered quickly and went into the same fighting routine as before John had has many fights in his time and he recognized a pattern in his attack. John was confirmed in his suspicious as the solider struck him in the same places on his body hurting him all over again. John fought him back scoring a few punches here and there he did not want to give away what his plan was. He waited for it, He waited for it, then it came a full round house kicked for his head trying to knock him out! John, did what was completely unexpected, he jumped on the solider like a spider monkey. He landed on him full body. John took advantage of his surprise, and grabbed him by the collar, and pile drive his face with his right handed power punches. One, two, three, the solider was done. John looked at him sprawled out and unconscious in his hands. John shook him and he was out like a light. John let him drop to the ground of the arena. He teleported back to his room took a long hot shower; he washed off the dirt and the grime of the previous encounter. While he was standing in the shower he could not shake the deniable feeling of dread. He thought to himself this guy is going to kill me if I don't kill him first. I cannot win them all. John contemplated that as he dried himself off and nursed his wounds.